NEED FOR SPEED™

BRIAN KELLEHER

BERKLEY BOULEVARD BOOKS, NEW YORK

THE BERKLEY PUBLISHING GROUP
Published by the Penguin Group
Penguin Group (USA) LLC
375 Hudson Street, New York, New York 10014, USA

USA • Canada • UK • Ireland • Australia • New Zealand • India • South Africa • China

penguin.com

A Penguin Random House Company

NEED FOR SPEED

A Berkley Boulevard Book / published by arrangement with
Dreamworks II Distribution Co., LLC c/o Striker Entertainment, LLC

For information, address: The Berkley Publishing Group,
a division of Penguin Group (USA) LLC,
375 Hudson Street, New York, New York 10014.

ISBN: 978-0-425-27388-3

PUBLISHING HISTORY
Berkley Boulevard movie tie-in edition / March 2014

PRINTED IN THE UNITED STATES OF AMERICA

10 9 8 7 6 5 4 3 2 1

Interior text design by Kelly Lipovich

**Part
One**

One

―――――――――

THE COPS WERE waiting for them this time.

When they were tipped that yet another illegal street race was about to take place in their sleepy little town, the Mount Kisco police had decided to go on the offensive.

The night watch commander had assembled three patrol squad cars whose sole duty would be to stop the alleged race. To this end, he'd equipped them with some extraordinary tools: three new highly accurate radar guns, three extra sets of walkie-talkies, and, borrowed from the New York State Police, a spike strip.

This device was composed of a collection of metal spikes, two inches long and pointing upward, attached to a rigid plastic strip. The idea was to throw the strip in front of any car that needed to be stopped and allow it to puncture the car's tires, grinding the lawbreakers to a halt.

It seemed like a drastic measure, but the police felt it had come to this. There was a culture of illegal street racing in Mount Kisco; most of the participants were local teenagers or young men in their twenties, and all were well-known to the police.

But no arrest could stick without catching one of the perpetrators in the act. Truth was, the street racers were all extremely skilled drivers and absolutely fearless. Their cars were highly modified with illegal equipment that made them go light-years faster than a normal passenger vehicle. In the past, the street racers had made short work of ditching any police cars that took up their pursuit.

Tonight, the Mount Kisco PD hoped to turn the tables.

The three extra squad cars were positioned along the illegal race's suspected route.

One cruiser was hidden in an alley in the downtown business district. Another was near the cemetery along Lexington Avenue, and the third was stationed next to the statue of Chief Kisco at the intersection of Routes 133 and 117.

The tipster had claimed the race would start at midnight. But it was at 11:55 p.m., five minutes early, that three cars came blazing into town.

They were a 1968 Gran Torino, a 1969 Camaro, and a 1966 Pontiac GTO.

They went by the first squad car so fast and so unexpectedly, the officer behind the wheel couldn't get his engine started quick enough. The trio of racers was gone before he even could get his squad car in gear.

Forced to call ahead to the second squad car, the policeman discovered his walkie-talkie was filled with static and interference. The same was true for his squad car's dashboard radio. As a result, he couldn't hear his colleague and his colleague couldn't hear him. It was almost as if someone was jamming their communications.

No pursuit was possible, because the first police car couldn't confirm where the three speeders had gone. The officer finally used his cell phone to call ahead to the second cruiser, which was lying in wait near the Lexington Avenue Cemetery.

But the three racers had already rocketed by this location as well—and the second squad car's new radar gun failed to register a thing. The three cars were suddenly there, going by at more than 100 mph, and like stealthy phantoms, were just as suddenly gone.

The second cop had seen the three cars only in a blur, but still he knew they were breaking a long list of laws: speeding, going down one-way streets, reckless driving, driving without license plates, and, most probably, carrying illegal jamming equipment.

All this second policeman could do was head off in the same direction in which the three fast cars had disappeared. But as soon as he pulled out of his hiding spot, he nearly collided with the first squad car, which had reached his position at almost the same moment.

All this time both officers had been frantically trying to contact their colleague in the third squad car to tell him the racers were probably heading in his direction and to drop the spike strip. But the interference on their radios continued unabated and communication seemed impossible.

As it turned out, the cop in squad car number three had heard the trio of racers approaching. The highly modified cars made a lot of noise when their engines were at full throttle. At that point he'd jumped out of his car and flung the spike strip across Route 117 right near the Chief Kisco statue.

Then he'd retreated behind his cruiser, not knowing what to expect once the speeding cars hit the spikes.

But that didn't happen.

Showing off their incredible driving skills, the three drivers simply avoided the spike strip by going up and over the curb and driving along the road's shoulder until they were past the tire-popping device. They did this while going in excess of 100 mph.

After that, the road straightened out and the three cars simply upshifted to their highest gear and were gone.

It was only later that the Mount Kisco police realized their tip had come from one of the racers themselves.

Being chased by the police was part of the allure of illegal street racing.

* * *

Mount Kisco was located in upstate New York, about ten miles east of the Hudson River, and just a half hour north of New York City.

With a population of ten thousand, the town was known as a bedroom community for high-price executives who worked in Manhattan, as well as a haven for the mega-rich. Secluded places like Guard Hill, Mount Kisco Chase, and Glassbury Court had homes so extravagant that only the fabulously wealthy could afford them. The downtown business district was made up mostly of designer bou tiques, posh clothing stores, foofy coffee shops, and expensive restaurants. And at close to two hundred acres, the Mount Kisco Country Club took up nearly one tenth of the town.

But Mount Kisco had a poor section, too. The Lexington Avenue neighborhood on the west side was home to families living below the poverty line. Most townies avoided the area, though this was where drugs could be bought. Local high school kids—pupils of nearby John Jay Prep school—SUNY students, and even some residents from the affluent east side were known to visit Lex Ave on occasion. Weed was especially easy to obtain there, usually at reasonable prices.

Still, the town's crime rate was very low. Since the police had so little to do, they frequently harassed the local teenagers at their hangouts, like the Applebee's on Main Street. And they especially enjoyed busting up underage drinking parties at Pride Rock and under the town's water tower.

Stopping the town's rash of illegal street racing, however, was still a work in progress.

There was an auto repair garage just north of downtown called Marshall Motors. It was a well-known place, having been in business for forty years.

It was a large, square, open building, with a washed stone facade, many windows, and a rather grand covered entrance reminiscent of a hotel. Signs on the outside advertised body work and tune-ups. There were four bay doors, plus room for many cars out front and along the sides.

On this day, a handful of cars were parked outside, all with various ailments, waiting to be serviced. Inside, a 2004 Taurus was on the main lift, getting its brakes redone. In the next bay over, a 2007 Neon was awaiting its inspection sticker. Next to the Neon, a classic 1970 Chevelle, stripped of chrome and glass and covered in primer gray, was about to go into the paint booth for its final coat.

The garage was a highly organized place, with hundreds of car parts neatly sorted on shelves and walls. Canisters of premium auto paint dominated one corner. The mechanics at Marshall Motors didn't just fix cars. They also painted them, restored them, and, if it was the right set of wheels, transformed them into street racers, packed with illegal equipment that could make them go very fast.

The employees of Marshall Motors were well-known to the police, too.

Mount Kisco had a different kind of economy when the garage first opened in 1974.

Back then, most people were making a good wage, and many families had two or more cars. When they needed an oil change, or an engine tune-up, or a dent pounded out, many of them came to Marshall's, and the business thrived.

But the money streams had changed in more recent years. As the town's rich got richer, they bought BMWs, Benzs, and Bentleys, and wound up bringing them to their dealers for service. Meanwhile, the poor got poorer and found they had to change their own oil or tune up their cars themselves—and forget about fixing the dents.

Caught in the middle, Marshall Motors had suffered, especially lately. Even the customizing work was tailing off these days. This morning, even though five cars were waiting to get in, there were a dozen empty customer parking spots outside, and two of the bays were vacant.

Business could have been better.

Photographs covered one wall inside the garage.

They showed a happy kid in various stages of growing up, always with cars around him. At four years old, he was smiling and posing in a bumper car at a local carnival. At eight, he was photographed racing go-carts, again wearing a huge grin. By ten years old, the boy was in a helmet, racing shifter cars. In these photos he could be seen holding all kinds of racing trophies, always smiling, always with his proud parents standing nearby.

But after that, the photos told another story. On his reaching eleven or so, the boy's mother was suddenly absent from the photos—and the boy was never photographed smiling again. He and his father appeared in half a dozen more shots, taken over the next ten years inside the garage while they were repairing cars, both stone-faced and lost in their work.

Then the photographs stopped altogether.

Four young men were inside the garage today; three of them were working.

One was Benny Garrett. He was a sunny African-American, and the possessor of a big personality. Benny was the garage's "gasser," or paint mechanic. His work was considered by all to be exceptional.

He'd been discharged recently from the army. While he'd originally joined the service to get out of Mount Kisco, where he went instead was Iraq and Afghanistan, as part of a helicopter ground crew. He'd seen how the muffler shops in Fallujah had been turned into bomb-making factories and how many Afghan farmers had their own working tanks, needed to keep thieves away from their poppy fields.

Very little of his time in the army had been cool or exciting, and he'd seen enough death and destruction to last several lifetimes. When he returned home after four years and three combat tours, he vowed never to leave Mount Kisco again.

But he'd also brought home with him a head full of stories about his time in the Sandbox. As he was always known for his vivid imagination, Benny's friends took these tales with a grain of salt. Just Benny being Benny.

In the next bay, making adjustments to the front suspension of the 1968 custom-built Ford Gran Torino, were the shop's chief mechanics, Joe Peck and Finn.

Joe was the oldest of the group, well into his thirties. He was a big guy, huge arms and chest, a fanatic in the weight room. With a dark face and dark eyes, he possessed a bushy, but well-defined, goatee, and more often than not, he had a toothpick hanging from his lips.

Joe had been at Marshall Motors the longest of the four. Having gotten a job sweeping up the place at the age of seven, he'd never really left. He'd learned the mechanic's trade from the business's founder and turned out to be one of the best grease monkeys in Westchester County.

Finn was the opposite of Joe. He was small, pale, with lighter hair and sad features. He was twenty-five and was the only one of the four who'd attended college. Although he'd earned a business and finance degree at a nearby

SUNY campus, he hated office life and never truly pursued a professional career. The day after getting his sheepskin, he was back at Marshall's, changing oil and installing shock absorbers.

The fourth young man was Little Pete.

Barely five foot four, he was aptly named. Fair-skinned with a James Dean haircut, he was a powerhouse in his own way. If he was considered the little brother of the Marshall Motors crew, he was also the most knowledgeable when it came to cars and racing, legal or otherwise. He was also an excellent driver and owned a very sweet 1969 Chevy Camaro that he'd reconditioned from the wheels up, practically by himself.

Pete was rarely seen without his iPad, and today was no different. It was 2:00 p.m. and his favorite streaming video show was coming on. It was called *Underground Racing*. It was hosted by a very nutty guy named Monarch.

The show was passionately devoted to the street-racing culture. Souped-up cars competing against each other on city streets and public highways at speeds frequently in excess of 150 mph. This was not drag racing run on a track and sanctioned by a thick rule book. This was about going as fast as you could go on an open road, with powerful but illegally modified cars, sometimes for money, but mostly for the adrenaline rush, which was always substantial.

Though the modern version of the sport began in

Japan, with enthusiasts racing each other on curving mountain roads, its history in the United States went back much farther. Back in the days of Prohibition, bootleggers jacked up the power of their car engines so they could shake off any pursuing law enforcement. Once booze was legal again, the bootleggers took to racing each other in their modified cars, and American street racing was born.

These days, technology and the right mechanic could take a typical consumer automobile and double, or even triple, its engine's output to 500 horsepower or more. But that was just the beginning. Ultra-expensive vehicles built especially for this sort of thing—Lamborghinis, Ferraris, and Bugattis—could easily double that figure. With these cars, speeds of 200 mph or more were not unheard-of, making them blurs to people keeping to the speed limit on interstates or simply driving on city streets. The "unapproachable" speed, the holy grail of street racing, was somewhere around 250 mph. That would be traveling one mile every fifteen seconds. Like breaking the sound barrier in a jet fighter, such velocity in a car could be exhilarating. But it took only one wrong move, and the person behind the wheel would, more often than not, wind up dead.

Monarch was the perfect host for the *Underground Racing* program. There was a great mystique about him. He broadcast the show from a secret location, known only to him. His viewers could see he was in a glass booth, with a microphone and camera in front of him—but little else. The only clue to his whereabouts was the occasional sound of seagulls his followers could hear cawing in the background, off camera.

Monarch was a real man of mystery—mystery and a bad heart. It was rumored that he'd had a dalliance as a professional race car driver but his heart stopped like a watch one day, so he quit. Legend also had it that he'd sponsored a few Formula 1 teams for races at top venues like Monte Carlo. But even here he was said to be highly secretive, always campaigning under assumed names.

Beyond that, very little was known about him.

Monarch's streaming podcast was private, by invitation only, and he was very discriminating about whom he invited to his party. Still, he had a huge, if discreet, following. Little Pete was one of his biggest fans.

"He's really on fire today," Little Pete said now, turning up the iPad's volume so the others in the garage could hear.

Suddenly, Monarch's voice was bouncing off the bay walls.

"Caller, listen, caller!" he was barking, fast-talking as always. "Did you just call me the Oracle of Delphi? The De Leon is my race and it's beautiful! And you can bet that crack in your ass that I *am* the Oracle of Delphi when it comes to who gets invited to race De Leon and who doesn't! So sew that crack cuz you're talking out of your ass and I'm not listening."

The four members of the Marshall team laughed. Monarch was the Howard Stern of the underground racing world. And he was one seriously funny dude.

"By the way, I have some local results," Monarch's voice crackled again. "The Flyin' Hawaiian just took down Steve Heavy Chevy in the Arizona desert. And the word is, it wasn't very pretty. Now remember that rivalry isn't over yet, you cretins. But the Flyin' Hawaiian *did* just get closer to an invitation to this year's De Leon as the wildcard. What's a cretin, you ask? If you weren't such cretins you'd know what a cretin is! De Leon is in one week, motorheads, so keep the need. Keep the motherfucking need for speed!"

The De Leon was the Super Bowl of underground racing. While the entrants were always hand-picked by Monarch himself, the participating cars were never less than the multimillion-dollar Lamborghinis, Bugattis, McLarens, and Saleens. The race was held in a different place every year, the location kept a closely guarded secret until shortly before it began. It was almost always a brutal, cutthroat competition whose winner, if there was one left standing, got to keep all of the expensive cars that managed to cross the finish line. The highly illegal race was always the bane of whatever law enforcement agency whose jurisdiction it happened to fall under, and street racing fans counted the days before the next De Leon would be run.

The Marshall Motors mechanics stayed entranced by the show even as they continued to work. All except Joe Peck.

As he looked through the glass doors of the garage, something caught his attention outside.

A sixtyish-year-old man in a business suit was talking to the garage's young owner, Tobey Marshall, the boy depicted in the photographs. Tobey was in his mid-twenties now, tough-looking but handsome and in good shape. He could've been a dead ringer for actor Steve McQueen.

But right now, Joe Peck sensed he had the weight of the world on his shoulders. Joe moved closer to the open bay doorway and tried to eavesdrop on the conversation.

"I loved your dad," he heard the older man telling Tobey. "He was a customer of our bank for thirty years, so this is very hard for me. But you're six months behind on the mortgage for this place and there's nothing more I can do to help you out. We'll have to foreclose on you if you can't come up with the payment next week."

Tobey didn't reply. He just nodded and awkwardly shook hands with the man. Then he watched in silence as the man got in his car and drove away.

As soon as Tobey walked back into the garage, he realized Joe had been watching the conversation—and maybe listening in as well.

"Who was that guy?" Joe asked him.

"Just an old customer of my dad's," Tobey replied quietly.

"I didn't recognize him," Joe said.

"He may bring his car in next week," Tobey added.

"Oh yeah? What's wrong with it?" Joe asked.

Tobey took a moment, and then replied a little testily, "It's our job to find out, right?"

Joe studied his friend for a moment. Tobey's father was the reason Joe was in this business. He was the one who'd hired him as a kid to sweep the garage, and in the process, taught him just about everything there was to know about what made cars run—and run fast.

"Is your mind on tonight's race?" Joe asked Tobey.

Tobey just shrugged.

"Well, I want to get there early," Joe continued. "Five cars are racing—so that means the pot will be like . . ."

"Like five grand?" Tobey said, finishing the sentence for him, and then adding a bit soberly, "Believe me, I know."

It was Tobey's car on the lift in the garage's first bay. Built in 1968, the Gran Torino fastback was a somewhat ordinary vehicle at its inception, though, like Tobey, many enthusiasts had embraced it as a platform for competing either legally or on the streets.

Tobey's Gran Torino was well-known to street racing fans in upstate New York and indeed throughout the country. He'd installed a rebuilt 5.4 liter aluminum big block engine in it with fuel injection and a supercharger. Huge headers, exhaust pipes, and twin mufflers were added to the package, along with a six-speed manual transmission and an especially heavy-duty clutch. The car sat on four radial drag-racing tires, mounted on old-school mag wheels, and had cobalt blue acrylic paint covering its body with white racing stripes added tastefully along the sides and atop the hood.

The paint scheme and the striping made the car look both unusual and elegant, but most important, it was fast. Stripped of any needless or extra weight, it could go from zero to 60 mph in under six seconds, astonishing for such an ordinary design. What's more, its suspension had been improved through the skills of Joe Peck and Finn, so that it cornered like a dream, and was also excellent at drifting—that manner of taking a turn not in the usual way, but by oversteering so that all four wheels temporarily lost traction, allowing the car to go into a turn sideways in a kind of high-speed controlled skid. In the world of underground racing, a driver's talent at drifting spoke volumes about the driver himself. Tobey was one of the best in the country at it.

That was one of the reasons Tobey was so well-known in the street racing community. All those years, from crash 'em cars to present, he had put to good use. He had an instinct about driving, almost a sixth sense. When he started his car, he felt it become a part of him, like some fighter pilots say when they climb into their airplanes.

And he'd always raced for fun. But now, after the visit from the man from the bank, he knew he might have to start racing for something more.

Two

━━━━━━━━━━

IT WAS SATURDAY night.

Traditionally, many of Mount Kisco's teenagers would cop some beer and head for Pride Rock for a drinking party.

But something else was going on tonight. Something somewhat secret. And it was happening at the Mount Kisco Drive-in Theater.

The sign at the drive-in's entrance was slightly misleading. It announced a car show, a ten-dollar entry fee, a BBQ, and some raffles. But something else was going to happen here. Something the cops hadn't been tipped about. People had started gathering inside the drive-in shortly after dark. Though scenes from *Bullitt*, one of the best car chase films ever made, were being projected on the drive-in's huge screen, the crowd wasn't on hand to watch movies, either.

They were there to see a real street race.

Or at least the beginning of one.

The drive-in's parking lot was jammed with spectators by the time Tobey arrived.

It was close to 11:00 p.m. and there was a drunken county fair atmosphere around the place. With everyone in good spirits, the crowd gladly parted to allow his Gran Torino to get through.

Inside his highly customized car, Tobey and his crew were tuned in to Monarch's show on Pete's iPad. They were about to get a big surprise.

The underground host had a caller on the line.

"Word is out that the De Leon is going to be held in New Hampshire this year," the caller said. "Is that true, Monarch?"

"*You'll* never know," Monarch snapped back at him. "Because you'd just tip off the cops—and no one wants that. No one likes a snitch! Am I right?"

The Gran Torino erupted in cheers.

"And, by the way," Monarch continued. "The results from Austin just came in. Texas Mike has posted a win."

Monarch took another caller. This one asked, "Why does Texas Mike have a shot at the De Leon and I don't?"

Monarch erupted. "Because Texas Mike's McLaren F1 is worth one point two million, can do 240 miles per hour, and he can drive!" he shouted. "And you and your rolling bucket of bolts can't. The Oracle has spoken!"

More cheers from the Marshall crew.

Monarch paused a moment, then went on.

"But, you know," he said, his voice unusually subdued. "Tonight I've got my nose open on Mount Kisco, New York."

This perked up the ears of everyone in the Gran Torino.

"You're shitting me," Benny breathed. "Did he just say Mount Kisco?"

The others shushed him as Monarch continued.

"I'm interested in that one-horse town tonight because Tobey Marshall and Jimmy McIntosh are gonna duke it out in a field of five cars," Monarch declared. "That's a real scrappy circuit up there, and from what I hear, Tobey Marshall is a hell of a driver. Just another Cinderella looking for a dress for the ball. But I'm serious. If Tobey ever gets a car worthy of his talents . . . he just might get an invite to the De Leon someday."

"Well, ain't that a bitch?" Finn said to Tobey. "First Monarch gives you a shout-out. Then he shits all over your car."

"You mean *our* car!" Peck reminded everyone.

Tobey shrugged. "That's just the way he is," he said.

He finally found a place to park the Gran Torino, and the Marshall team climbed out.

Suddenly Little Pete stopped in his tracks, closed his

eyes, and acted as if he was receiving some kind of message from the Great Beyond.

He turned to Tobey. "While Monarch was talking about you just then, I had a vision."

"Here we go," Finn murmured.

"Quiet," Benny said with a laugh. "I love hearing the kid's visions."

Little Pete began: "I saw water and the sun and—"

". . . and your sister in a hot bikini?" Finn interjected with a laugh.

"Shut it!" Little Pete scolded him. "This is serious."

He composed himself and continued.

"I saw Tobey in this vision," he said. "And you know what? He's gonna win the De Leon."

"No shit?" Finn said with good-natured sarcasm. "Tobey Marshall is gonna win the crown jewel of underground racing? Against McLarens and Bugattis and . . . Wait—is this going to happen this year?"

Finn was right. Small illegal street races happened all the time, and they almost exclusively involved cars that were customized stock cars anyone could buy, such as Camaros, Mustangs, or Gran Torinos. But again, the De Leon was at the other end of the rainbow, involving high-end foreign-built cars like Lambos and Buggs. If any American-built cars were involved, they were usually soni-cally priced Mustang GTs and maybe, on an odd-moon Monday, a Chevy Corvette. But that happened very rarely.

As was usually the case, it was a question of the haves and the have-nots. If Tobey had been able to recoup the sweat equity he and the others had put into his Gran Torino, its price tag might reach twenty grand or so. The cars that raced in the De Leon—their tires cost that much.

Still, Tobey appreciated Little Pete's enthusiasm.

"Thanks for your vote of confidence, Pete," Tobey said. He'd just spotted his main competitor for the night: the driver named Jimmy McIntosh. "But I'll have my hands full just trying to beat Jimmy."

Tobey nodded to McIntosh's tricked-out 1966 Pontiac GTO, just pulling into the lot.

It was a beautiful car. Dark blue, 383 boosted engine. Holly quad carbs, big tires, big rear gears, and an enormous exhaust system.

But Tobey's friends were looking in the other direction.

"What the hell?" Little Pete whispered.

A Mercedes SLR had driven into the parking lot. This was a very luxurious car. It was silver, low-slung, and shaped like some kind of futuristic bullet with four huge wheels attached. When seen in the company of Ford Gran Torinos and Pontiac GTOs, the SLR was doing some serious slumming. Only a limited number were built every year, and its price range was north of half a million dollars.

The car attracted a lot of attention as it pulled to a stop in the center of the crowd, not just because of its notoriety but also because of its driver.

"Shit, is that Dino Brewster?" Little Pete said, not wanting to believe his own words. "What the hell is he doing back here?"

Dino Brewster . . .

They had all known him for years; Tobey had gone to high school with him, though they'd been at different grade levels. Dino was in his late twenties now, built like a professional athlete, and handsome. He was one of those people who always had perfect hair, perfect smile, perfect car. Perfect everything.

He'd also been one of the richest kids in town. Though it was never really clear what his father did for a living, or even if his last name was really Brewster, Dino always had money, always had a new, bitchin' set of wheels, always had the best clothes.

And he always stood out. In a school where most kids wore jeans, hoodies, and T-shirts, Dino always wore black—almost like a Goth with access to an expensive wardrobe. He was always a real douche bag, too, arrogant and mouthy—but many girls just couldn't resist him.

Tobey and Dino had been at odds since the first moment they met as young kids. They were just different in many ways. Tobey was down-to-earth, working class, and reluctant to talk about his accomplishments. He didn't mind getting his hands dirty. Dino looked like he'd never done an honest day's work in his life—and was proud of it.

An interest in cars was just about the only thing they had in common; this had also led to their many disagreements.

They'd had one fistfight, though there could have been many more. The skirmish happened in the locker room after gym class and Tobey gave Dino a definite beat down. But no one else was around at the time of the battle; there were no witnesses. So Dino lied and told another story of the clash. Because of this, the exact winner of the fight was always in dispute.

Tobey had very few problems with other people around town. Townies, Goths, metalheads, nerds—he could get along with just about anyone. But what he didn't like—in fact, what he detested—were liars and braggarts, and that was Dino in a nutshell.

But Dino also had the infuriating talent of being able to convince lots of people that his version of the truth was the right one. That's what made him so devious. Even people who had been burned by him in the past could fall for it again. That's how good he was. And those suckers would usually realize what had happened only when it was too late, after Dino had gotten what he wanted from them.

Tobey had raced Dino many times over the years, during high school and beyond. And no matter what luxury car Dino was sporting at the time, Tobey always beat him—at least that was not in dispute.

But as time went on, Dino had been able to work 24/7 on his driving skills, while Tobey had to just plain work. Because of his family's wealth and his father's connections, Dino had had the opportunity to practice endlessly at driving high-end cars while other kids his age were forced to work at McDonald's.

Dipping into his father's apparently unlimited pool of

money, he was also able to afford driving lessons from some of the top names in the business and get practice time on some of the largest racetracks in the Northeast.

Most important, though, Dino was able to call on his father's friends in the racing world to get him into key races. Small ones at first, then intermediate, and then finally on the senior circuit.

This was no big surprise as he fit the bill. He had movie star looks, drove very expensive cars, could afford a good support team, and had plenty of sponsors.

All this, and always with a good heaping of daddy's money, was how he got to race in the Indianapolis 500.

In the car culture in Mount Kisco, only Dino had reached that pinnacle.

For now . . .

Having Dino arrive for the night's meet was a major buzzkill for the Marshall Motors crew. It brought their lighthearted conversation to a sudden halt.

And it only got worse.

Soon after the Benz parked, its passenger's-side door opened and an attractive female stepped out.

She had long brown hair, big eyes, and a gorgeous shape. She radiated slightly as she mixed with the crowd standing around the car, standing out in the throng like a light in the dark.

This was Anita, Little Pete's sister. Around town, the adjective usually applied to her was "smoking."

Tobey felt his heart sink on first seeing her. He and she had a past; one that didn't have a happy ending.

Anita had been Tobey's girlfriend through most of high school and for a few years afterward. They were an "it" couple—they were almost always together, and when they weren't, they were always texting each other or yapping on the phone. They'd spent so much time together that there was a time when they would finish each other's sentences, to the annoyance of their friends.

They knew each other's families well. They'd climbed Mount Kisco many times. Had eaten numerous times at Applebee's. Had drunk beer at Pride Rock. It was there that they had their first kiss and their first sex. As a couple, they had been happy, witty, and fun to be around.

But throughout their relationship, deep down, Tobey knew that they were actually different people. They wanted different things and had different dreams. His dreams resided within Mount Kisco's area code. To continue his father's business and to build it into one of the best customizing shops in the country—a hope that was fading fast. Her dreams went about forty-five miles south, to the glamour of New York City, leaving the small-town life behind.

So they broke up. She moved to Manhattan and Tobey carried on. But not a day went by when he didn't think about her, and about what might've been.

And now this. Dino and Anita . . . together.

It was the perfect storm of misery for Tobey: his ex-girlfriend showing up with his hated rival.

"I'm sorry, Tobey," Little Pete told him. "She didn't tell me she was coming home."

"It's okay," Tobey said, trying to convince himself that was the case.

But it wasn't.

A crowd quickly gathered around Dino's luxurious Mercedes. Meanwhile Anita had walked a few steps away from the impressive car, and as she did, the crowd quickly closed in around Dino. Many were young motorheads who'd fallen for his charm. They all wanted to take photos with him and his car.

Strangely, with the way Anita was dressed—in a slinky, low-cut, green dress and sexy mid-calf boots—it almost seemed like she was just another of those young fans lost in the swarm—and not Dino's date for the evening.

"Do you think he's here because he wants in?" Finn asked, watching the little drama unfold. "You think he wants to race?"

"Screw him," Benny said. "We're not letting a four-hundred-and-fifty-thousand-dollar Mercedes into this race."

"Try six hundred thousand," Joe Peck corrected him, painfully admiring Dino's car. "And that's *before* the modifications."

"Maybe he just came to watch how a real race driver drives," Finn said boldly. "Maybe he'll learn something here."

But Tobey just shook his head at the chatter.

"That guy raced Indy," he told his friends. "It doesn't get any more real than that."

"Yeah," Joe Peck said. "But he only lasted a season and a half at Indy."

"In other words, he sucked," Benny said.

But Tobey just kept shaking his head.

"He made the top five in three races," he said. "He didn't suck. Far from it. He knows what he's doing."

"But you've got to remember," Joe Peck said, "he wrecked a guy under a caution flag—that's about as low as you can get. That's why they banned him."

Again, that was Dino all over.

Finn turned to Little Pete. "Telling us that your sister was 'kind of' seeing Dino Brewster was one thing," he said. "But actually seeing that she is seeing him? That's totally different. That's a real mind fuck."

"It's a nightmare is what it is," Little Pete said gloomily.

Meanwhile, the lovefest around Dino continued unabated. He signed autographs with the patience of Hollywood's friendliest leading man. Smiling and laughing nonstop, he posed for pictures with the locals. At one point, he tried to pull Anita into some of the photos, but she posed only reluctantly. It was all she could do just to keep smiling.

While the Marshall crew couldn't take their eyes off the little scene, Tobey was more affected by it than the rest. But none of them liked it.

"If your parents had the cash his parents did," Joe Peck said to Tobey, "you'd be racing open wheel, too."

Tobey just shrugged. Who knows?

"And you'd be beating him," Finn added. "Just like you beat him every time you guys went head-to-head."

Tobey shook his head again. This one went deep.

"Not every time," he said sadly.

He was looking at Anita when he said this—and now she'd spotted him across the parking lot. Their eyes met. Hundreds of emotions flowed back and forth, slow-motion electricity bouncing between the two of them.

She broke the spell by giving him a little wave. All he could do was nod back to her.

That's when she started walking in his direction.

"Oh, shit," Joe Peck said. "This can't be good."

The gang immediately surrounded Tobey.

"Let's go, man," Finn said, trying to get Tobey out of her line of sight. "You don't need the distraction."

But Tobey shook his head again.

"It's okay," he said. "It's cool."

But his words didn't convince anyone—including himself.

Joe Peck turned to Benny. "You better get going, dude," he told him, checking his watch. "The race is gonna start soon."

Benny smiled and swung his arms behind him as if they were wings.

He began to sing, "I believe I can fly . . . I believe I can touch the sky . . ."

With that, Benny "flew" off, pretending to be some kind of human, singing bird.

Benny being Benny.

A moment later, Anita arrived.

She was even prettier up close, but was very shy as well.

"Hey guys," she said sweetly. "Hey, Petey."

"Hey," Little Pete replied, almost under his breath. He hadn't seen her in a while.

They hugged, and Anita asked him, "Are you racing tonight?"

"Yep," he replied curtly.

"Well—be careful, okay?" she told him sincerely.

Pete just nodded. Then Anita turned toward Tobey. The rest of the group took their cue and wandered away. Tobey and Anita were alone.

She touched his arm, just for an instant. But it sent a jolt through him.

"Hi, Tobey," she said, trying to smile.

"Anita," Tobey said with a nod, trying to stay cool.

"I was really sorry to hear about your dad," she said softly. "You got the flowers, didn't you?"

Tobey nodded again—this was very uncomfortable. There was a long pause. He stared at the ground, and Anita stared at him. She had stopped trying to smile. The look in her eyes said it all. She should've stayed with him . . .

Anita broke the silence. "Thanks for watching out for Pete," she said.

Tobey just shrugged. "Glad to do it. He's like a little brother to me."

Her smile returned briefly.

"How's the shop?" she asked, trying to sound cheerful. Truth was, it was harder for her to talk to Tobey than it was for him to talk to her.

"Fine," Tobey lied. "Everything's going good . . ."

Anita was a little surprised to hear this. "Really? Well, that's nice . . ."

She was trying her best to hide the skepticism in her voice. There was another awkward silence. Now it was Tobey who broke it.

"So how's the big city?" he asked her.

"Different than I expected, I guess," she replied. "But it's not here, that's for sure."

Tobey forced a smile. "You still allergic to Mount Kisco?"

Anita almost laughed. "You still think you're funny, huh?" she said. "Well, I'll tell you. There's a few things left in Mount Kisco that I really like."

Tobey shook his head a little. "Seems like you found what you're looking for."

Anita knew what he was talking about: Dino.

"I'm taking it real slow," she said, almost like she had to convince herself.

Tobey looked her right in the eye.

"Dino's not a guy who takes anything slow," he said, carefully pronouncing every syllable.

She glared right back at him. "Then you should have moved a little quicker," she scolded him.

A third awkward silence—but this time their eyes were locked on each other.

"Is that what you came here to tell me?" he asked her in a harsh whisper.

She shook her head. "No—it isn't," she replied. "In fact, Dino has something he wants to talk to you about. Something important."

"I doubt that," Tobey said.

"It's true," she said. "But not until after the race. I don't want to distract you."

Tobey had had enough. He said to her, "Then you should've stayed in Manhattan."

With that, he walked away.

It was almost midnight.

Joe Peck was standing under the Mount Kisco overpass, the finish line for the upcoming race. Crews for all of the cars competing in the race were standing nearby.

Finn was also there, working on his laptop.

Joe's cell phone rang. It was Tobey, still back at the drive-in.

"What's your status?" Tobey asked him.

"We're in place at the finish line," Joe replied. "How are you feeling?"

"I'm okay," Tobey told him. "Do you have the road locked down?"

"Well, Benny is up there," Joe said. "Or at least I think he is. Hold on . . ."

Joe Peck pushed a button on his radio handset.

"Liar One?" he called into the mic. "Are you standing by?"

Benny's distinctive voice came through the handset's tiny speaker.

"Not this again," he moaned. "Why do you have to use that shitty handle?"

"I wouldn't have to use it," Joe Peck told him, "if you would just stop telling people you flew Apache helicopters when you were in the army."

"I was a mechanic in army *aviation*," Benny replied testily. "And I once took an Apache for a joyride. That's all I ever said."

This *was* an impressive boast, however, which is why the others in the Marshall Motors crew had their doubts about it.

Apaches were the most powerful combat helicopters in the world. An Apache was like a tank with a rotor spinning on top. They could carry hundreds of pounds of bombs, missiles, or rockets. Each was also equipped with a massive gun, a weapon that could put some serious hurt on just about anything. An Apache could definitely ruin your day if you were on the wrong end of its weapons.

But it was not just what they were packing that made Apaches so fierce. The copter could fly nearly 200 mph, could do loops (rare for any helicopter), could stay aloft for hours, and in general could mimic a lot of maneuvers jet fighters were famous for doing. Only the cream of the army aviation's crop were qualified to fly them.

Again, while he was a great guy, Benny was known to

exaggerate, and since he'd come back from the military, his tall tales seemed to have grown even taller. This was why his buds were skeptical about his claim to have gone joyriding in an Apache.

"I know that's what you said," Joe Peck told him now. "It's just that I don't believe you."

Benny's exasperation came through loud and clear. "Just because I was a copter crew chief, that doesn't mean I don't know how to fly a chopper," he said.

"All right, Liar One," Joe Peck said, emphasizing the last two words. "Whatever you say. Now, please, what's the status?"

Benny *was* full of dubious claims, but at least one of them was true. He *could* fly an airplane. That's where he was now. Inside a Cessna Skyhawk, flying above the proposed racecourse.

While the Cessna Skyhawk was definitely not an Apache, it did take some skill to fly one. It had a big engine, could fly more than 150 mph, and at more than three miles high. While the Cessna was among the most popular airplanes ever built, only a pilot who knew what he was doing could fly one safely at night.

Benny looked out over the controls of the Cessna, studying a small TV screen showing a night-vison view of the racecourse below. The race would be run on public streets, but the course itself wasn't strictly about driving fast on straightaways. Almost half of the course would take the drivers down some of Mount Kisco's narrowest back alleys and side streets; places with lots of sharp corners and tight turns. How to get through this rat's maze quickly was part of the overall strategy—and danger—of the event.

Benny's job up here was to be on the lookout for the police, or civilian cars, or any kind of vehicle that might get in the way of the race. This was critical, as the speed of the cars involved might go as high as 140 mph.

"It's looking good," Benny finally reported. "Looks like most of Mount Kisco has gone to bed."

"Okay, Liar One," Joe Peck responded.

"Hey, you got a death wish, Pecker?" Benny yelled at him. "My call sign is 'Maverick.' Got it? Call me Maverick, or—"

"Or what?" Joe asked, laughing.

"Or I'll kamikaze this bird right into your nut sack," Benny replied.

The start of the race was just minutes away.

Back at the drive-in, Tobey pulled a wad of cash from his pocket and counted it quickly.

One thousand dollars. This was a lot of money for him. The mortgage on the garage. Providing paychecks for his crew. Ordering supplies and car parts. Keeping the electricity on. The thousand dollars might have been put to better use.

But Tobey had suddenly found himself in survivor mode. Just seconds before his father died, Tobey had promised him he'd do anything and everything to keep Marshall Motors going. And so, desperate times called for desperate measures. He knew it was time for him to put his skills as a driver to better use than just getting a rush at 150 mph. He knew it was time for him to keep his word to his father.

He counted out the cash one more time and then joined the other racers in a circle near the race organizer's station.

This was going to be a box race, a well-known event in underground racing circles. It was simple. A predetermined entrance fee was put into a box by each racer. Whoever won the race won the contents of the box.

One of the race organizers was holding the box.

"Everyone knows the rules," he told them. "There's no handicapping in this race. No set-out lengths. You'll leave from a standing start; first bumper to cross the finish line wins."

Tobey thought about it for just one more moment. Then he threw his money into the box. The other four racers did the same.

They would be formidable opponents. Jimmy had his balls-out GTO and Little Pete would be driving his beautiful '68 Camaro with its 427-cubic-inch Corvette engine. A cute girl named Jeny B would be driving a very sweet Porsche 944 coupe with a 3.1 liter, heavily modified 300 horsepower engine under its hood, a powerhouse for such a small car; and a guy named DJ would be driving a BMW 3.0 E9 with a 3.2 liter engine bumped up to 310 horsepower, again, a lot of power for such a tiny featherweight burner. Tobey knew none of them would be a pushover.

With the money in place, the race organizer handed Tobey five playing cards.

"Do you want to do the honors, Marshall?" he asked Tobey.

"Why not?" Tobey replied, shrugging.

The race was going to start with the cars lining up in two-car rows. The selection of the cards determined where the racers would line up.

Tobey checked the playing cards. They were all Clubs, from the ace to the five card. He held them face down and gave them a quick shuffle.

"Okay?" the race organizer asked the others. "Everyone agree the cards are clean?"

They all nodded.

"Okay, Jimmy," the race organizer said. "You pick first."

Jimmy McIntosh selected a card. He turned it over to reveal the two of clubs.

"Not bad," he said with a smile.

Little Pete went next.

He crossed fingers on both hands, seemed to say a quick prayer, then picked his card. It was the ace.

"Yes!" he shouted. "The spirits are with me!"

Because Little Pete had picked the ace, and Jimmy had the two card, they would comprise the first row, one-two.

Jeny B went next. She selected the three of clubs.

"Could be worse," she said.

Now it was just DJ and Tobey, and Tobey was not feeling the love. He'd hoped to get a start closer to the front, but that was impossible now.

DJ drew the five of clubs and his shoulders slumped badly. Tobey didn't feel much better, as that left him with the four card—in other words, he would start out in the second row next to Jeny B.

It was better than being last like DJ—but not by much.

"Okay, that's done," the race organizer said. "I suggest you get to your cars quickly so we can get this bad boy up and running."

Tobey dialed Joe Peck while he was walking back to his car.

"Fourth pick," he told Peck when he answered. "Second row, next to Jeny."

He heard Joe groan on the other end.

"Where's Petey at?" he asked Tobey.

"That little son of a bitch picked the ace," Tobey reported with dark humor.

"Well, at least it's still in the family," Peck replied.

"I know," Tobey said. "But it ain't his garage we're trying to save."

"Okay, you don't need me to tell you this," Joe counseled him. "But you're just going to have to pick your spots. Bide your time, and then push in the dagger when you see the opportunity. During the rest of it, just stay cool."

"Roger that," Tobey replied.

Tobey hung up and Peck relayed the position news to Finn.

"Not a disaster," Finn said. "He's overcome worse."

Besides putting Tobey's Gran Torino in its best

condition ever, the Marshall crew had also installed a video camera on its front bumper. Anything the cam saw would be beamed to Finn's fired-up laptop. This way, the crew would be able to see every move Tobey made. It would be like going on the ride with him.

Finn pushed a few keys on the laptop, and in an instant they were looking at the video image being transmitted live from the race's starting point back at the drive-in. After a few bouts of static, the signal locked in and the picture became extremely clear. It showed what was left of the crowd in the drive-in parking lot—many of them were now heading for the finish line—as well as the ghostly images of nearby lights, glaring weirdly in the night.

Once the visuals were set, Joe Peck once again activated his air-to-ground radio handset. He called Benny.

"Status?" Joe yelled into the handset.

"Still all clear," was Benny's reply. "No cops. No civilians. No one in the way at all."

This was good. In races like this, it was always better for all concerned if the course was "clean."

Crews for the other four cars were nearby. Joe yelled to them: "Our eyes in the sky says it's all clear. Time to rock and roll."

But suddenly Joe felt the hair on the back of his neck stand up. He turned to find Dino Brewster, of all people, standing behind him. It was as if he'd come out of nowhere.

"Go away," Joe told him.

"Not so fast, Joe," Dino replied. "We're all brothers here—brothers of the wheel, right?"

"I don't know anyone who'd want to be your brother," Joe shot back at him.

But Dino just laughed. He pointed to Finn's laptop and the live feed from Tobey's bumper cam.

"Mind if I take a look?" he asked.

"Can't you afford one of your own?" Finn asked him bitterly. "Why are you bothering us?"

Dino just shrugged. "I left my laptop in my other Mercedes," he said. "You know, the SL550?"

Any other time, that would have been enough for either Finn or Joe to level Dino, or at least cuff him upside the head. But other things were happening here. This wasn't just another race. There were high stakes involved. If Tobey didn't win, Marshall Motors, their home away from home for many years, would probably be no more.

Plus the race was about to begin.

So this was not the time to start a brawl. This was time to pay attention to the big picture and let the little things ride.

With much reluctance, they let Dino watch the race with them.

Back at the starting line, located on the road just outside the drive-in theater's entrance, Little Pete had expertly maneuvered his Camaro next to Jimmy McIntosh's Goat, making up the box race's first row.

Jeny B slid her Porsche in side by side with Tobey's Gran Torino, completing the second row. DJ's BMW 3.0 filled out the line in the third row.

On a signal from the race organizers, the drivers began revving their engines. The sound quickly became deafening, like the roar of distant thunder. Exhaust smoke and blowing dust filled the night air. Each driver gave a thumbs-up—they were all ready to go.

Then the five drivers focused their attention on something off to the right. Their muscles became tensed and unmoving. They were all hair-trigger nervous. For good reason.

Off in the distance, a freight train was approaching. Its dull mechanical growl grew rapidly, the cry of its oncoming whistle cutting through the night.

Suddenly it came around the bend at Battery Hill. Its ultrabright front light slashed through the darkness.

At the very moment its beam appeared, the combined revving of the five engines hit its peak.

Then, tires began to spin. More smoke rose into the air. The noise decibels reached the maximum. One of the race organizers dropped a handkerchief and all five cars suddenly exploded off the line.

Little Pete had the best start—it was almost *too* good. His Camaro shot into the first right-hand turn, reaching it way before anyone else.

But he took this first corner too aggressively, drifting much farther out than he wanted and almost spinning into a ditch. It was only a slight delay, but even a moment's loss could be costly in these types of races. As proof, Pete's miscue allowed Jimmy McIntosh to get the inside line. Jimmy laid on the gas and quickly gained a lot of ground on Little Pete.

Meanwhile, just two seconds behind, Tobey, Jeny B, and DJ drifted violently around that first crucial corner as well, but with a little more control.

A short downhill straightaway lay ahead.

Beyond that was a railroad crossing.

A mile to the north of the race's starting line, CSX freight train Number 12, traveling from Wassaic, New York, to Oak Point Terminal in the Bronx, was running right on schedule.

The train consisted of thirty-two freight cars being pulled by two massive diesel locomotives, each boasting 4,000 horsepower. The Number 12 was traveling at 55 mph at the moment, its average speed, and was due in the Bronx at 12:35 a.m.

As it cleared Battery Hill, it reduced its speed to 45 mph, but only temporarily. After the bend there was a gradual decline that ran for several miles. Once the train reached this stretch of track, its speed would increase to 65 mph, its fastest for the entire eighty-two-mile trip.

As running trains was all about staying on time, this increase in speed was built into Number 12's thrice-weekly schedule. So, just like every other time this midnight train passed through Mount Kisco, it was due to cross the open road intersection at Chase Avenue, arriving there at precisely 12:05 a.m.

The railroad crossing was only a mile from the Mount Kisco Drive-in, near the end of the appropriately named Railroad Street. The crossing had many warning lights and an alarm bell that rang to high heaven whenever a train was approaching. It also had a standard St. Andrew's caution cross on a high pole looking over it and a street-level sign that advised all to "Look Both Ways."

But Chase Avenue was a passive crossing. It had no crossing gates. It was located in such an isolated spot, on such a little-used road, the New York transportation department had long ago deemed crossing gates unnecessary.

At 12:04, the crossing came alive. Its red lights began flashing and the warning bell began ringing madly. But none of the five race drivers, now just a quarter mile away, lifted off their accelerators when the commotion began.

Just the opposite. They were all heading as fast as they could toward the railroad crossing.

Not unlike Tobey's Gran Torino, the train crew had a video camera attached to the front of their locomotive. Unlike Tobey's bumper cam, though, the train's video setup was equipped with infra-red night vision capability, allowing the train crew to see any unusual heat sources that might be looming in their path for up to a mile away.

And at the moment, the train crew could see five extremely bright blobs of heat traveling at high speed down Railroad Street, heading right for the crossing.

"Those punks!" the engineer cried. "Not again!"

Suddenly the night was cut by a sound that drowned out even the roar of the five race car engines.

It was CSX Number 12 blowing its collision horn. The train crew had seen this type of thing before—crazy kids in souped-up cars playing chicken with their train. They knew how insanely dangerous it was. That's why they were laying on the emergency horn so long and loud, even as the race cars were just seconds away from reaching the crossing.

But the horn had no effect. None of the racers showed any signs of slowing down. If anything, they were trying to go faster.

Little Pete's Camaro was the first to streak across the railroad crossing.

He hit the raised track bed so hard and so fast, he went airborne for a few long seconds. Then he came down just as violently as he went up, crashing back to the asphalt roadway. But his extra heavy-duty shocks cushioned the blow just as advertised, and he was unharmed. Pete shifted down just one level, to get back some of the speed he'd lost while in flight, and then booted it again. He was soon back up to 110 mph and still solidly in first place.

But in these kinds of races, being solidly in first place

was just a matter of inches. Jimmy McIntosh's GTO had been right on Pete's bumper, when Pete went flying over the tracks, and by mimicking Pete's maneuver, Jimmy went airborne, too.

He landed, just as Pete had, hard and fast, bottoming out a bit, but causing nothing more than a brief storm of sparks before regaining form. Pushing his pedal to the floor, he reclaimed his solid second position in an instant, gluing himself to Pete's ass.

Just seconds behind them were Jeny B and Tobey. They were neck and neck as they approached the railroad crossing, traveling side by side in excess of 100 mph. But Tobey was in the dead man's slot. He was closest to the oncoming train and if something went wrong, it would hit him first.

The locomotive's extremely bright headlight blinded him as it filled up the interior of the Gran Torino. It was like the sun itself was coming through the passenger's window. But there was no turning back now—and Tobey knew it. There was no way he could stop in time; no way he could swerve out of the way. He had to either beat the train or get crushed by it.

He roared across the raised tracks a heartbeat later, Jeny B going over just an instant before him. Both of them went airborne. Though she was a hairbreadth in front of him, had the train hit Tobey, she would have been killed an instant later as well.

But none of that happened. They both cleared the tracks—and the rush that went through Tobey's body was like nothing he'd ever felt before. He'd never been that close to being killed in a race or anywhere else. He'd come within mere inches of being obliterated by the train, but in this race within a race, car versus locomotive, he'd won.

He and Jeny hit the pavement at the same time, creating a twin storm of smoke and sparks. At that moment, Tobey looked over at her, his face lit by the sparks they'd both just created. He was surprised to see her glancing back at him, the same look of exhilaration and relief on her face as he was sure was on his.

Their twin expressions said it all . . .

This is why we race.

DJ was still in last place, though.

Doomed by his poor placement at the start, he knew as soon as he saw the first four racers go over the crossing that there was no way he could make it in time.

Everything happens fast while traveling at 110 mph, sometimes faster than the human brain could process. DJ was just twenty feet away from the railroad crossing when CSX Number 12 reached it. Its emergency horn was still blaring, yet DJ was still heading straight for it, seconds away from colliding with it. He pulled on his emergency brake, instantly locking his brakes. But this was not enough. He was still going way too fast to avoid disaster.

In the next instant, he turned the BMW's wheel

violently to the right, propelling him into a ragged drift which, in among a lot of smoke and dust, put him driver's-side-first with the train—*not* where he wanted to be. Desperate, he put both feet on the brakes and went into a full skid. He turned the wheel violently again, this time to the left, causing him to drift wildly in the other direction. He turned 180 degrees and came to a stop so close to the crossing that his side mirror was hit by the passing train. The mirror exploded into the driver's window, sending shattered glass all over him.

It all happened in just three seconds—and the first thing DJ did was check his crotch. It was not wet, thank God; not even a little moist.

He was out of the race, and out $1,000. But at least he was alive—and dry.

Now there were just four—and they were racing practically two-by-two, bumper to bumper, down the rest of Railroad Street.

They came to a sharp corner. Little Pete and Jimmy went into a drift side by side, but Jimmy's GTO got wobbly as his outside wheels hit the dirt.

He tried to correct the problem, but was forced to dive right. Cars were parked on the shoulder of the road and he was just seconds away from smashing into them.

Tobey and Jeny B saw what was happening and tried to take advantage of the situation. With Jimmy in trouble, they both powered themselves around the corner at the same moment, almost making it three wide. But Jimmy was a great driver. He recovered quickly and was back up on the street in a flash. He immediately split between Jeny B and Tobey, almost smashing Tobey's right front quarter panel in the process.

Tobey shook his head in frustration. Jeny B had managed to get ahead of Jimmy and claim second place, but Jimmy's astute driving had not only shut the door on Tobey—it had pushed him back into fourth place.

But Tobey had a plan.

He knew there was a tight turn up ahead. It was a hard corner to the right that went through a small concrete tunnel, followed by an immediate left. Tobey strategically moved wide, putting himself on the outside and in a good place to take this first sharp corner. Then he waited.

Still in the lead, Little Pete drifted through the turn with precision. Jeny B was now right behind him. But as she entered the right-hand turn, Jimmy's presence right on her bumper forced her to overdrift. She lost control for a moment, bouncing her car off some debris that had been stacked at the tunnel's entrance.

This slowed down Jeny B just enough to let Jimmy move back into second place. Meanwhile, his plan foiled, Tobey had been forced to brake through the tunnel to avoid the falling trash.

When the smoke cleared, he was still in fourth place and unable to make up any ground.

*   *   *

The four cars jumped onto Route 16, a straight and narrow highway, and finally opened up their engines for some real high-speed driving. All four were soon roaring along at 140 mph–plus.

They blew through a desolate intersection like they were all moving at the speed of sound. Then they came to an underpass with just microseconds separating them. Each car rocketed through it, closing in on 145 mph. Beyond them now was the small, quiet city of Mount Kisco.

But then came trouble . . .

At that moment, up in the Cessna, Benny had spotted something.

He quickly clicked his microphone on.

"Be advised . . ." he said, "I have traffic ahead. Repeat—I've got traffic ahead!"

Still on the highway, the four drivers were approaching a wide intersection when Tobey got Benny's call.

All were still going close to 150 mph and it was then that they saw the first signs of life. There were a few civilian cars driving about, creating some light traffic on the highway.

This didn't concern Jimmy or Little Pete. They blasted by the cars like they were standing still, drifting wildly and going through the next intersection sideways.

Jeny B was not so lucky. She had to swerve to avoid one of the civilian cars and began spinning out. This was the opportunity Tobey had been waiting for. He hit the gas and threaded the needle between Jeny B and a civilian car.

And just like that he was in third place, leaving Jeny B behind.

Waiting at the finish line, Finn was following the race on his laptop. Joe Peck was watching over his shoulder. So was Dino.

They'd watched the bumper-cam image of Tobey drifting through the potentially dangerous intersection and then accelerating madly into third place.

"That was a close one," Dino said. "He got lucky there."

"That's not luck," Joe Peck shot back. "Our boy Tobey is patient. He waits for his moments."

Tobey was always in total control, and Finn and Joe knew it.

But Dino only laughed.

"Sure thing, guys," he said snidely.

It was ten past midnight and the streets of downtown Mount Kisco were deserted.

But not for long.

The roar of the oncoming race cars sounded like a

formation of jet airplanes approaching; the thunderous noise was soon echoing off the locked-up buildings of the sleepy downtown.

With Jeny B crapped out, there were only three racers left. Jimmy was now in the lead. Little Pete was right on his bumper. Very close behind was Tobey. This was where the race changed radically. Gone were the straightaways. Now the route brought them through a warren of back alleys and narrow streets in the older part of the tiny city.

All three of them loudly drifted into the first alley, the cacophony of screeching tires reaching new dimensions. The alley, behind East Main Street, was narrow, and once in, there was no way to pass. At this point, it was more like driving through an obstacle course than a race, but all three drivers handled it expertly.

Seconds later they bounced out of the alley, roaring across Boltis Street and into the next alley beyond. Sparks were flying everywhere; their undercarriages were tearing up the old asphalt pavement. But none of the three dared slow down.

Out of the second alley, they came to a hard left turn onto St. Mark's Place. Though it was not much wider than the alley, all three were screaming down it in seconds, topping 100 mph.

Little Pete was able to regain the lead coming out of St. Mark's Place. Jimmy fell behind because he'd drifted too wide but was still a close second, with Tobey right behind him in third.

This was okay. Tobey's reputation was one of patience and opportunity. His talent was knowing when to make a move and his genius was not stressing about it if that move failed, because more chances were always right around the corner. And at that moment, rocketing down that side street, Tobey decided to make a move.

He mashed his accelerator, and an instant later almost collided with Little Pete while trying to outflank Jimmy. An instant after that, they all slid sideways into the entrance of a place called I-beam Alley.

All three of them did a violent drift, which evolved into doing a U-turn while screaming past a huge parking structure. Pete was driving in such a way that he was almost able to control Jimmy's steering, countering him move by move. But by doing that, Pete was also preventing Tobey from getting around both of them. It was highly successful and very ballsy driving for the little guy. As a result, they left I-beam Alley in the same positions as when they went in.

Now they were back out on a somewhat wider thoroughfare, this one called Spring Street. From here they accelerated toward a statue located in the center of the town square, that of "Chief Kisco." All three of them drifted around the statue into a right U-turn, but Jimmy had gained the prime lane. He hit his gas and in a burst of power was able to sneak in front of Pete.

Again, the noise was either awesome or bloodcurdling, depending on your point of view. But once around the statue, they headed for the two-lane Route 117 beyond it.

All three immediately went into the left lane. This was another point in the race Tobey had been waiting for. Time to try another move. He jerked his steering wheel sharply and dove into the right-hand lane. His main objective was to get past Little Pete.

And he was about to do it, when up ahead, a very slow-moving street sweeper filled Tobey's field of vision. It was completely blocking his path. There was only one thing he could do. He red-lined his RPMs, upshifted, and then dropped the hammer just shy of the max. In that instant, he closed the gap between Little Pete and the street sweeper. Then he counted down.

"Three . . . Two . . . One . . ."

At the very last moment, Tobey floored it, shot in front of Little Pete, and screeched back into the left-hand lane all in one smooth motion.

Just like that, he was in second place.

He took a moment to look in his rearview mirror. Little Pete was now right on his tail, furious that Tobey had so expertly jinked him, especially after Jimmy had done the same thing to him just moments before.

"Sorry, little buddy," Tobey called out, with a smile. "Them's the breaks."

A few seconds passed—then all three screeched into another alley, this one off Moore Avenue. They were back in the rat's maze at top speed, but Jimmy hit his gas a little too hard and sideswiped a brick building just a few feet down from the alley's entrance. This slowed him just enough for Tobey to get right on his bumper.

Tobey felt like he was moving at warp speed inside the alley and up ahead he knew it would begin to widen. Time for another move. He jerked the wheel violently to the left, taking the outside lane, hoping to start his turn out of the alley early, and thus gain even more on Jimmy.

The three cars shot out of the alley a few seconds later, screeching left onto Woodland Avenue, which was a one-way street. Tobey's maneuver had worked; he'd gained the inner lane and was now in a good position to try for the lead. But coming out of nowhere, he saw a homeless man who was pushing a shopping cart step off the curb and right into his path.

Tobey was boxed in so tight by Jimmy, he had no other choice but to drive right into the shopping cart.

The cart exploded into a million pieces the instant he hit it, sending debris up and over his car. Seeing the remains of the shopping cart flying through the air, Little Pete swerved at the last possible moment, barely missing the rain of rags and junk.

That was way too close, Tobey thought.

He screamed into his radio:

"Benny!"

Benny replied just as quickly.

"I saw you had it, bro!" he said. "No worries!"

The three cars drifted loudly left onto Poplar Street

only to find a civilian car in the oncoming lane heading right at them.

Tobey took the opportunity to inch just a little closer to Jimmy's bumper, leaving Little Pete behind. This position allowed Tobey to draft off Jimmy as they started to pass the approaching car together.

Once again, Tobey decided to make a move. Once past the civilian car, he swung onto the wrong side of the road. He was now down in third gear; his engine was screaming. He shifted up to fourth; his engine screamed again, but the move served to slingshot him around Jimmy's left bumper. Tobey buried his accelerator and was instantly neck and neck with the GTO.

Suddenly they were approaching the arched underpass, the finish line lit by flares.

This was it.

The underpass went by in a blur. Tobey poured on everything he had. Just as they exited under the overpass, he did a quick look to his left and saw the grill of Jimmy's car not six inches behind him.

A second after that, it was over.

Tobey had won.

But there was no time for celebration as Benny was suddenly screaming into his radio: "Doughnut convention!"

His warning needed no translation, but Finn provided one anyway.

"Cops!" he yelled.

On that word, the racers, their cars, and their crews simply vanished.

When, a few moments later, a police car arrived at the finish line, siren blaring, lights flashing, the only things left were a few burned-out, but still smoking, flares.

Three

THE SOUNDS OF beer cans being popped and loud hip-hop music filled the night air around Marshall Motors Garage.

The race had been over for hours but the crew was still talking about it, reliving it turn by turn. Joe Peck and Finn were especially excited when telling their version of events, as seen through the Gran Torino's bumper cam. As they talked while the Budweiser flowed, it was almost as if they'd been behind the wheel instead of Tobey.

Tobey and Little Pete listened to it all with good humor. They were standing side by side, as was usually the case. Tobey was Pete's idol, and Pete really *was* like a little brother to him.

"I thought you were going to catch Jimmy for sure," Tobey told Pete as he counted his five-thousand-dollar winnings again, one wrinkled bill at a time.

"I had him in the turns, but he's a hell of a driver," Little Pete replied, draining a beer. "And so are you. But I'll get you both next time."

It went on like this for a while. But Tobey was waiting for the right moment to steal away. Finally, he told the others he had to take a leak.

He walked to the far corner of the garage and looked up into the night. He was finally breathing normally again, his heart rate back where it should be. He'd been in street races before, but nothing as intense as this one. Maybe it was because there had been so much at stake this time.

The five thousand dollars would help. But he knew it was just a Band-Aid—a way to keep the wolves away from his door, but only for a short while.

Then what?

The bills would not stop. The bank would still want its money. And he couldn't expect his crew to work for free. He had to think of some other way to get income, or the garage would be history.

He was a good driver, but he was stuck in the minor leagues. Five-thousand-dollar box races were rare in his area. If he wanted to get in on others, he'd have to go to Chicago, Miami, or LA—hotbeds for these types of things. But the costs of traveling around so much would take away a big chunk of whatever he won. And maybe he wouldn't win all the time. Or at all. And how would the garage stay running if he was gone for long periods of time?

There was only one solution he could think of. He had to move up to the major leagues somehow. Play with the big boys—the guys who were getting slots in Monarch's De Leon. Trouble was, he couldn't do that in his Gran Torino. He would need to have a real supercar, or at least drive for someone who owned one.

He knew Monarch had been right on the money earlier that evening. If he got ahold of a good car, maybe the De Leon wasn't so out of the question.

But until then, he was stuck down here in the bushes.

He looked out over the town's skyline. All was quiet again in Mount Kisco. He could just barely see the outline of Pride Rock against the starry sky. He wondered how many happy, drunk kids were still up there, stumbling around in the dark, as he had done many times in the past. He hadn't been up there in years. Like it or not, it was a place that belonged in the memories of his early youth.

Besides, he could never think about it without thinking of Anita. She'd looked so beautiful earlier at the drive-in. He missed her terribly. They were two different people, on different trajectories, different paths. But, damn, he loved being with her.

He'd always carried a quiet confidence about him, a trait inherited from his father. And while he knew his decisions might not have always been right, at least he knew that he thought carefully about anything important before he proceeded.

Except when it came to Anita.

The more that time went on, the more he'd become convinced that he might have really blown that one.

He walked back to the garage, grabbed another beer from the cooler, and fell back into the never-ending bullshit session about the race.

But suddenly, a noise from outside distracted them.

Finn got up and looked out the window.

"You've got to be shitting me," he said. "What the fuck is *he* doing here?"

"Who?" Peck asked.

"How many assholes do you know that drive a Mercedes SLR?" Finn asked.

"All of them," Peck replied in perfect deadpan.

"Oh, yeah," Finn replied, then said, "then, how many of them are named Dino?"

They heard a car pull up a moment later. Through the bay door windows they could see it was in fact Dino's Mercedes SLR. No one said a word. They watched as Dino got out of the car and looked around the outside of the garage, sniffing at the grease and grime. Then he headed for the open bay door.

As one, the crew stood up and formed a united front at the threshold. There was no way they wanted Dino to enter the garage itself. This was their turf.

Dino spotted them and immediately stopped in his tracks.

He looked at Little Pete.

"That was some nice driving out there, short stuff," he said, sucking up. "I'm impressed."

But Little Pete just laughed at him.

"You hear that, Tobey?" he said. "Dino Brewster is impressed with me. I can die happy now, I guess."

Tobey glared at Dino, but said nothing.

Dino smiled thinly. "And there's Mr. Tobey Marshall," he said. "The man to beat in Mount Kisco . . ."

Tobey looked him up and down, but still said nothing.

"Sorry about your old man," Dino went on, in a very patronizing fashion. "I know you two were close."

Finally Tobey spoke. "Are you lost or something, Dino?"

Dino had to think a moment.

"What do you mean?" he asked.

"You haven't been around here in a long time," Tobey told him acidly. "Figured you must be lost."

Tobey took a step toward Dino to emphasize his words and make one thing clear: He was not wanted around here.

"So nothing's changed then, Tobey?" Dino asked him. "Even after ten years you still want to just pick up some locker room fight?"

But Tobey wasn't really looking at Dino. He was looking at the Mercedes, searching for any sign of Anita.

"She's at her folks'," Dino told him, reading his mind. "This has nothing to do with her."

Tobey felt his shoulders droop. But at least she wasn't with Dino.

"So what do you want, Dino?" Tobey finally asked him. "We're busy here."

"It's simple," Dino said. "I want to see you build a real car."

Tobey waved him off. "I got plenty of cars to build."

Dino took a look around the rough-edged garage. "Yeah, well, how's that been working out for you lately?"

Tobey gave him a hard look. Dino shrugged.

"Listen, Tobey, I didn't come here to insult you," he said, a bit of his attitude seeming to disappear. "I came here to make you a business proposition, something that could be a game changer for you."

"You handing out dreams now, Dino?" Little Pete scoffed at him. "How much is this going to cost us?"

Dino ignored him. He looked around the garage again.

"I've seen a hundred custom racing shops since I left this town," he said to Tobey. "But I still haven't seen work as good as yours."

The garage crew was silent. None of them knew what to make of Dino's compliment.

"That's all the work of these guys," Tobey said, pointing at the others. "That's not me . . ."

Dino took a breath. "Let me get right to the point," he said. "I've got a very special car that needs to be finished."

"What kind of car are we talking about?" Joe Peck asked.

"A Ford Mustang," Dino replied.

"A Mustang?" Joe said. "There's only about a million of them out there."

"But not one like this," Dino told him. "It's the last Mustang Ford and Carroll Shelby were building before Carroll died."

Suddenly everyone in the crew was paying rapt attention. Carroll Shelby was not only a rock star in the world of customized cars, he was considered the Godfather of street racing. To say he was an automotive genius was like saying the sky was blue or the sun was hot. Invoking his name was no little matter.

"Thousands of people would want to put their hands on a car like that," Tobey said. "How did you get it? You steal it?"

Dino ignored the insult.

"Mr. Shelby and my uncle were close friends," he explained. He waited a moment, then continued, "Here's the proposition: If you finish building that Mustang like you rebuilt your Gran Torino, I'll give you a quarter of what I get when I sell it."

Little Pete exploded.

"A quarter?" he exclaimed. "You cheap bastard!"

"If it's done up right, the car will be worth two million, minimum," Dino shot back. "That will be five hundred thousand dollars in your pocket."

The crew fell stone-cold silent. That kind of money had never been anywhere within their reach before. Dino and Tobey just stared at each other. There was a lot of history between them, all of it bad. Where was all this going?

Dino broke the silence. "I look around here and I see a ton of talent and no opportunity," he told them. "Face it, you guys are dying here. I mean, it's obvious. So just forget everything that's happened between us. That's ancient history. I'm here to make peace. And money—for all of us."

Tobey's crew exchanged worried looks. Each one knew this was wrong—trading with the enemy. The uneasy silence could have been cut with a knife.

Dino went on. "Look, don't answer me now, Tobey," he said. "Just think about it."

As Dino turned to leave, Tobey looked back at his crew. He already knew their opinion on this.

But then Tobey just shook his head. "I don't need to think about it," he said suddenly. "I'll do it."

A gasp came up from the others.

Dino smiled. "I'll have it here tomorrow," he told Tobey.

There was no handshake. No good-bye. But Tobey and Dino exchanged a brief look of nonhostility, if not respect.

Then Dino got back into his Mercedes and drove away.

Someone turned off the music. The beer cooler was closed. An angry silence now enveloped the garage. Benny finally broke the spell.

"I have one question for you, boss," he said to Tobey. "Have you lost your fucking mind? We're going to work for Dino Brewster?"

Joe Peck stood up. He was the oldest one among them, their elder statesman.

"Yeah, what the hell, Tobey?" he asked. "You don't want anything to do with that asshole."

"He's a bad guy," Finn added. "And he's always been a bad guy."

Benny spoke again.

"We don't need that jackass, boss," he said. "If this is about Anita, and getting her back, do that a different way, homie. Write a poem or some shit. 'Dear Anita . . . nothing is sweeter than Anita. I really "anita" Anita . . .'"

The crew laughed—all except Tobey. But Finn pushed on.

"Forget Dino," he urged Tobey. "Tell him you're out. We're doing fine here without him."

"But we're not," Tobey said, stunning them. "We're not doing fine."

The crew was surprised to hear this—except Joe Peck. The conversation he'd overheard earlier suddenly made sense.

"Well, many people are hurting, Tobey," Finn said. "You know things have changed in this town. It's a tough economy for everyone. Or mostly everyone."

Tobey thought for a moment.

"Look. I'm way behind on the loan," he finally told them. "The guy from the bank was here today. Ask Joe— he saw him."

Joe Peck could only nod and stare at the floor.

"They're going to shut us down," Tobey went on. "It's as simple as that."

This was a crushing blow for all of them to hear. They loved the garage and everything that went with it.

Little Pete spoke up. "Look, I hate Dino as much as anyone else here," he said. "But if what you're saying is that we need to work with him to save this place, then I'm with you, Tobey."

But Finn still disagreed.

"You just made five grand tonight, Tobey," he said. "You're not completely broke."

"That's got to be enough to make your loan payment," Joe Peck added.

"But what happens next month?" Tobey asked them. "And the month after that? I can't expect to win all these dinky races. Even if I did, it still wouldn't be enough. You're the business major, Finn. You know what I'm talking about. It's a question of dollars and cents, and a steady flow of income. And we just aren't getting that anymore."

This was serious, and they could all feel it.

"Here's the bottom line," Tobey told them. "If we don't do this, then this place is gone."

He looked at each one for a long time.

"Anyone here up for that?" he asked.

No one said a word.

The next day a flatbed truck pulled up to the front of Marshall Motors.

Behind the wheel was an individual appropriately named Big Al. Obese and sweaty, he was Dino's right hand man.

He backed the truck up to the garage's main door.

On the back was a car that looked vaguely like a

Mustang, but it was sitting on blocks and many of its key components were missing. It was far from being a completed car.

It was in such a state of disassembly it took a while just to get it off the flatbed and into the garage.

But once that was done, the doors of the garage were closed behind it—and from that point on, Marshall Motors would never be the same again.

Part Two

Four

THE FIRST THING the Marshall Motors crew did in the Mustang rebuild project was treat themselves to a steak dinner.

It was an easy decision. Shortly after taking possession of the Shelby Mustang, they found an envelope stuck in the driver's-side sunshade. Inside was a credit card from one of Dino's father's businesses. An attached Post-it note read, "For all reasonable expenses . . ."

The crew immediately piled into Tobey's Gran Torino and headed for Applebee's, where all five ordered the most expensive item on the menu: the 12-ounce New York strip steak. As they drank a never-ending stream of beer, they sat in a corner table and, keeping their voices down, mapped out what they wanted to do, and more important, what they *had* to do, to make the whole thing work.

They quickly realized their number one priority had

to be security. This was for several reasons. First, although they were now, improbably, working for Dino, they still didn't trust him. They knew it would not be beyond him to claim the gang had stolen the ultra-exclusive, one of a kind car. His visit to them after the box race had been caught on the garage's security cameras, as had Big Al's delivery of the Mustang itself the next day. Still, they knew they had to be careful and document everything just in case it was all an elaborate ambush set up by Dino.

Secondly, considering that the car they were going to build might have a price tag of $2 million or more, they needed to make sure everything they were doing stayed not just on the down low, and not just below the radar. Their activities had to be off the radar completely.

Again, this was just an exercise in playing it smart. They were well aware that there were some people in the local street racing culture who, if they heard something big was happening at Marshall Motors, something involving the late god Carroll Shelby, wouldn't think twice about breaking into the garage and stealing whatever it was. They also didn't want word to leak out to the underground racing media, Monarch included, because that might bring the same unwanted attention on a national scale.

So what they needed was security on a military scale. That's why they gave the job to Benny.

They spent their first full day of work on the rebuild closing down and sealing off two of the garage's four repair bays. The excuse, for anyone who asked, was that they were repairing and then repainting them. To this end, they draped blue plastic tarpaulins around the two bays, stretching them from ceiling to floor. They taped newspaper around the two windows that could look into the cordoned-off bays, and randomly sprayed some paint on the newspaper to make it look like they were in fact doing some painting within.

Next, Benny upgraded their security cameras to include an audio pickup. Then, he installed an upscale burglar alarm that came complete with infrared capability and motion detection equipment. He did all of this without advertising the upgrade by applying warning stickers on the outside doors and walls. They all agreed: If they were going to catch someone sneaking in, they wanted to do it quietly, so they could deal with it the same way.

Benny also advised them to not talk to anyone about what they were doing, even in a peripheral way. Loose lips sink ships, he told them over and over—and they knew completely buttoning up on the project would be in their best interest. They would continue doing business as usual at the garage—changing oil, giving out inspection stickers, doing tune-ups. They would work on the project mostly at night and into the morning, before the dwindling number of customers who still frequented the place showed up.

They even put into place a system where any overly exotic part that they needed, something not usually used in a typical civilian car, would be bought only from a rotating file of online dealers, as opposed to ordering it through the local NAPA auto parts store. That place, they knew, was a potential nest of spies.

Benny was so precise that he even came up with a system of how they would dispose of parts and used debris that could be traced back to the Shelby. Instead of throwing it all away in the Marshall Motors Dumpster, providing valuable clues to what they were up to, he had them load it all into garbage bags, which he then disposed of at various other Dumpsters around town.

As he told them many times, "This is how the CIA would do it."

They worked out a schedule of two men on, two men off, with Pete being the swingman. Two mechanics would be on hand during regular business hours to do the everyday Marshall Motors grunt work, while two would come in after closing and work on the supercar—which had been put up on the lift in bay number three—through the night.

Little Pete showed up whenever he was needed, or at least that was the plan. In reality, he was there almost all the time, day or night. Next to Tobey, he put in the most hours on the project, as he knew it might lead to one of his visions actually coming true.

But in the end, the car was Tobey's baby. He frequently did double duty, working the garage during the day and then working the project all night. When they got near the end, to the point where they didn't have to work continual nights anymore, Tobey still stayed at the garage, sleeping next to the Mustang-in-progress, baseball bat always within reach, keeping watch.

By that point, he didn't want to leave it alone even for a minute.

The first thing they had to do after the car arrived was, surprisingly, get rid of a lot of the stuff that had come with it.

As beautiful as the overall design was—or had been intended to be by the late, great Carroll Shelby—by the time the car got into their hands, it had a lot of stock and inadequate equipment attached to it. Just why this was, they never found out. It might have been from a previous attempt to bring the car to life, or maybe someone else's stab at security, hiding the jewel under a bunch of cheap parts.

But whatever the case, a lot of it had to go.

The wheels, the tires, the driveshaft, even the reconditioned 302 engine, all went in the trash. Getting rid of the 302 was especially painful. It was a sweet motor, but way below the standard they needed to make their vision run. Plus they didn't want to hold on to anything that could link them back to the unique Shelby. So everything from the brakes to the axles, from the differential to the exhaust, and even the gas tank, was taken off, cut up into little pieces, and put into garbage bags for Benny to drop off all over the area.

Next, they needed a real engine, something befitting what they were trying to build. As everything was being paid for by Dino's credit card, the Marshall crew didn't care about expense. As long as it worked, they weren't going to be concerned where the green was coming from or how much of it they spent. They just had to keep hard and fast documentation on everything in case Dino reverted to his usual devilish ways.

So after doing some research they purchased a 5.8-liter Ford all-aluminum DOHC engine with aluminum heads. Once this powerhouse was on-site, they installed forged aluminum pistons and rods and attached a treated forged crankshaft to it. Everything went smoothly.

The cylinders went in next, after they were coated with plasma arc iron oxide to reduce friction. Then came the supercharger, a high volume oil pump, and a dry sump oil system, all bought online from Japan. They machined the heads to improve valve action, and even polished their interiors to get better airflow. Then they put in four high duration camshafts and eight huge fuel injectors along with special high volume fuel lines to keep the juice flowing when they needed it.

After fitting on long tube exhaust headers, it came down to the spark plugs. It took Tobey an entire day online trying to figure out which spark plugs to buy, and once they arrived, what their proper gapping width should be.

But once all these things had been done, the entire gang gathered inside bay number three, crossed their fingers en masse, and turned the temporary ignition switch. The engine came to life with a roar so loud, their heads hurt for days.

They didn't mind a bit, though. It was music to their ears.

Though the engine still needed some tweaking, right out of the gate it began running at more than 6,000 RPMs, which they determined could translate to almost 750 horsepower, with a potential of 900. This, they knew, could mean the completed Mustang might reach a speed somewhere around 230 mph, an astonishing number that would have impressed Carroll Shelby himself.

In any case, it was an amazing achievement for the five glorified grease monkeys from Marshall Motors. They'd set out to create a monster, and that's exactly what they did.

But most monsters come with problems, and theirs was no different.

All the undercarriage work went well. They stiffened the chassis with heavy steel sub-frame connectors and installed top-of-the-line adjustable shocks and springs. They put a heavy-duty battery in the rear quarter of the trunk and installed a huge fuel pump plus booster and an overly large exhaust system. They thought the hardest task would be modifying the steering column to accommodate their gear shift paddles, which were installed on the steering wheel, eliminating the need for a stick shift and a clutch. But all that went well, too.

Then it came time to put in the driveshaft. They'd purchased one from the best dealer in the country, and had high hopes for a smooth installation. But no matter what they did, the custom shaft just would not fit.

They didn't know why. They'd checked and rechecked their measurements. Everything seemed okay. They checked their clearances—but again, nothing was askew. They spent three straight days and nights trying every way they knew to get the shaft connected, yet nothing worked. They even machined down the ends of the very expensive shaft, hoping to gain a few precious millimeters, but once again, it was no soap. And because they'd designed that portion of the drivetrain to fit this particular exotic driveshaft, there was no alternative out there for them to buy to replace it.

So they had to invent one.

Joe Peck and Finn pulled an all-nighter at the height of the crisis, and when Tobey came in the next morning, he found them both asleep or passed out—it was hard to tell which. But on the workstand was a new, completely original driveshaft they'd constructed out of carbon fiber material.

Tobey was astonished. They were all good at connecting things to cars, putting on parts bought from manufacturers, and making them go. But to manufacture something like this on their own?

He woke Joe long enough to have him swear the new driveshaft fit and would work. And as a bonus, it would lighten the overall weight of the car, a very important factor.

After a few hours' rest, they put the new piece of equipment to the test—and sure enough, it fit perfectly and ran perfectly.

It was that morning that Tobey knew something very special was happening inside Marshall Motors.

The brake work came next—never a favorite for any mechanic. But while it went slow—attaching fourteen-inch six-piston disc brake calipers and brake pads in the front and thirteen-inch ones in the back—it also went well. Everything worked after just a few adjustments. The wheels came next—hugely expensive, but critical, as they would have to hold on tight to the *enormously* expensive racing tires the crew had bought.

But that's when their monster became cranky again.

It happened the day they put the engine inside the car—this was to be a huge step toward completion. After weeks of working on the motor and the body separately, now the car would be getting its 700 horsepower–plus heart.

The engine went in fine—but when they tried to put the hood on, it was a no-go. The supercharger they'd installed was just a little too big and the hood they'd purchased a little too small. It just wouldn't close.

They tried every adjustment they could think of, including lowering a lot of the gear sitting on top of the engine, but it was futile. The fucking hood just would not fit. Of all the things to go wrong, they never saw this one coming.

Now what? They'd waited four weeks for the custom-made hood to arrive. They couldn't bear waiting another month for a new one, even if they could find one to fit.

So Joe Peck and Finn went back into their mad-scientist mode—this time with Tobey helping out. It took twenty-four hours straight of hard work, but they fashioned a completely new hood, once again from carbon fiber, making it sleek and workable.

It was then that Tobey thought, *Maybe we're actually getting good at this.*

Everything ran smoothly after that—at least for a while. The electrical system went in with no problems. The same was true for the fuel lines, the wiring harnesses, and the cooling system.

It was a happy day when all five of them pitched in to mask off the car for its primer coats, and then, with Benny as the main artist, spraying on its gleaming silver and blue finish.

When Tobey asked his gasser just how much the paint cost, Benny replied, "Only a gazillion dollars."

But the results were worth it. Once put together and painted, the Mustang looked so sleek and so aerodynamic,

NEED FOR SPEED 81

it seemed to be traveling 100 mph even as it was standing still.

They brought in a Chassis Dyno and programmed the FMU computer with software to maximize horsepower and torque. The program recommended ways they could get additional horsepower. They made these adjustments and were floored when the computer told them they were now in the area of 900 horsepower—which had been their holy grail since the beginning.

They finally celebrated that night. Before this, they had banned all beer, all booze, and all of any other kind of recreational distractions that might interfere with the project. But this milestone called for at least a case of beer—they were very close to finishing this awesome car, something started by the Godfather of it all. And they had done it in secret, off the radar, with no interference from Dino (who never once contacted them during the building process), with no break-ins, no fistfights, no tantrums.

Then, as one of the final elements, they weighed the car. The Dyno program had mandated it had to be less than 3,800 pounds, not including the weight of the driver, to get to that hallowed 230 mph. But when they put it on the scale, they discovered it weighed 71 pounds over that magical 3,800 number.

This was a real problem. They had been economical weight-wise when deciding what to put in their super machine. Now it was so tight, that anything they took off would have an undue effect on something else. With that came the danger that the whole thing would snowball into negative territory.

It all came down to numbers: If they wanted the 900 horsepower, to reach the mythical speed of 230 mph, they needed to lose 71 pounds.

But where?

It was Little Pete who unwittingly came up with the solution. He had been climbing around in the back seat of the car, trying to find something they could jettison to make it lighter, when he happened to say, "This back-seat is so small, even I'd have a hard time getting laid in it."

It hit them all at once. Why did a car like this even need a backseat? It wasn't like it was going to be used for double dates.

It took them another twenty-four hours to take out the backseat, along with all its braces and the heavy floor-board it had been sitting on. But once they filled in the empty space with yet more carbon fiber sheets, they weighed the car, and it came in at 3,794 pounds.

The Dyno computer program loved the result. They ran the program three times and each time it indicated that if everything stayed the same, they would have their 230 mph once the car made it out onto the road.

When they opened the doors to the garage that morning, it was barely 5:00 a.m.

Still, they rustled up some more beer and bought breakfast sandwiches from McDonald's to really celebrate. But when they sat down in the squeaky office chairs for their congratulatory breakfast, each one of them leaned back just to clear his head and wound up falling asleep.

The sandwiches grew cold and the beer got warm, but it didn't matter.

The weeks of work, the long nights, looking up from the welding machine to see the sun rising. Trash cans full of empty energy drink cans and power bar wrappers.

Their work was done.

And finally, they could rest.

**Part
Three**

Five

MANHATTAN WAS GLOWING brighter than the fantastic city of Oz.

Lights, buildings, people, cars, movement everywhere. The center of the universe—all less than an hour's drive from Mount Kisco.

While it might have seemed a million miles away for some residents of that small upstate town, at least a handful of them had made the trip down here tonight.

On the corner of West 51st Street and 6th Avenue, its entrance practically hidden between two empty storefronts, there was an art gallery that was so exclusive, so upper end, it didn't even have a name. It was meant to be a magical place, designed to instill wonder and awe, and when all the bells and whistles were in gear, for the most part, it worked. The high walls, the subtle lighting, the muted tones, the barely perceptible pulsing soundtrack. On special nights, a very fine mist would be released from the ceiling and would very gently rain down onto the gallery. It gave everything a golden sheen without getting anything wet, the droplets like little pieces of jewelry falling from the sky, or at least from the rafters.

This was one of those special nights.

The no-name space was filled to capacity. Several hundred of New York City's rich and powerful were rubbing elbows and drinking Brut Gold champagne. An invitation to this happening had been extremely hard to get—other events in the city this night paled in comparison.

At the stroke of midnight, those attending had their attention steered to a fantastic 3-D holographic program projected in the center of the room. Through spinning, moving drawings of mechanical designs and schematics, they were presented with the inner workings of the "last Shelby Mustang" come to life. The engine, the chassis, the interior, the wheels. Each component had not just been designed, the ghostly, disembodied narration claimed, but had been hand-sculpted in a way to fit together, altogether perfectly. And many of them were parts that were built only to exist within this fantastic machine alone, never to be made again.

Those gathered were appropriately enthralled, but there was more. When the narration concluded, the holograph began spinning faster, and suddenly it was like something ethereal was being born right before their eyes. This birth was represented by the image of a galloping stallion slowly transforming itself into the Mustang-inspired supercar.

The crowd applauded lustily, but still, the best was yet to come. At the same moment the horse morphed into the 3-D car, a curtain lifted, a fanfare came from nowhere and suddenly before their eyes was the magical car itself. The last Shelby Mustang. The Ford Supercar GT, displayed like a work of art, surrounded by plush velvet ropes.

Paparazzi camera flashes lit up the crowded room—the strobes of bright light bounced off the descending mist, now transforming them into millions of tiny emeralds, floating down, silently cascading onto the Mustang below.

It was like a psychedelic experience, without the drugs.

As intended, the crowd was beside itself with wonder.

In one corner of the room, though, looking very out of place and by no means caught up in the wonderfulness of it all, were Joe Peck and Finn. Both were dressed up, sort of. Peck was wearing an overly large jacket, a too-tight dress shirt, and even a tie, though its knot was done all wrong.

Finn looked no better. He'd borrowed a suit from a cousin, who obviously hadn't bought a suit since the mid-eighties. He and Joe had spent an hour before the show opened figuring out how to remove its massive shoulder pads without tearing any of the outer material.

They were extremely uncomfortable. Manhattan was

like another world to them. It was a big, noisy, expensive place that they never had any reason to go to, grand as it seemed to be. As soon as they'd stepped off the Metro-North train in Penn Station earlier that day, both of them would have given anything to be somewhere else.

Tobey and Little Pete weren't faring much better. They were standing next to the velvet ropes surrounding the supercar, also dressed in ill-fitting suits, a sea of beautiful people swirling around them. To them, the guests were like a different kind of species altogether, graceful and flowing, but plastic—and no matter what Tobey and Pete did, no matter how they stood or how they talked, they just couldn't blend in. They were sticking out like sore thumbs.

Tobey in particular felt out of place and lost. While he was proud of what they had done with the Super Mustang, this was not his turf. This was where Anita lived, and that alone filled him with negative, brooding thoughts. Eight million people called New York City home, but it was knowing that just one of them was here, within the city limits, and maybe even close by, that was enough to dishearten him.

He was so low that even at the very moment his supercar was being introduced, he caught himself thinking that he'd never felt so alone.

But then he met Julia.

When Tobey first spotted her walking across the room toward him, it was suddenly like she was the only person in the room who was in color—everyone else had turned to black-and-white. She was beautiful. Blonde. Well-dressed. And she moved with such confidence and grace; that in itself was a thing of beauty.

She reached the spot where they were standing, gave them both a visual going-over, and then asked, "So, this car—how fast does it go?" Her accent was British and very sexy.

"Fast," Tobey replied, just barely croaking out the word.

"*Very* fast," Little Pete added.

But the beauty was skeptical. It showed on her face, and especially on her lips.

"Aren't all Mustangs fast?" she asked.

"This car was built by Ford," Pete said, recalling words from the gallery's press release. "And reimagined by Carroll Shelby, the greatest performance car builder in American history."

"But, Pete," Tobey interrupted with a smirk, "that means nothing to her. Can't you tell? She's not from around here. And I doubt that she has any idea who Mr. Shelby is."

Pete thought a moment, but then concluded boastfully, "Well, we finished it. Our shop was the one that made a supercar out of it."

"Why is it so fast, though?" Julia shot back at him.

Pete smiled and went off script.

"Nine hundred horsepower, baby," he said. "Pure stroke and power."

Tobey had to laugh at Little Pete's exuberance—his little brother.

But still she was not impressed.

"Is that a lot?" she asked. "Nine hundred horsepower, I mean?"

Little Pete couldn't believe what he was hearing. "Are you kidding?" he asked her.

Tobey intervened again. "Relax, Pete," he said.

He turned to the pretty blonde.

"Miss, this isn't a car you can buy at the mall," he said. "Trust me when I say it's one of a kind."

Still she seemed confused.

"Can I see the engine?" she asked innocently.

Little Pete popped the hood with pleasure. Tobey raised it so she could see beneath.

"Huh . . ." she said, studying the engine closely, "5.8-liter. Aluminum block. Supercharger. Racing headers. Nice, actually . . ."

Little Pete just stared at her. He was speechless. Tobey, though, was smiling.

"Gotta admit," he said to her, "I wasn't expecting that."

She moved just a bit closer to him.

"From a woman, you mean?" she asked. "Or is it because I'm British? Mr. Shelby's first Cobra was built using a car called an AC Ace Bristol—manufactured in England. But . . . you knew that, right?"

Tobey fell speechless. There was nothing he could say to her at that moment that would have made any sense.

"Life can be full of surprises," she told him with a wink.

Little Pete piped up again. "I find life to be full of

people who think they're smart just because they have a British accent."

She turned toward him. "Is that right?" she asked.

"You ever watch Piers Morgan?" he asked back.

She giggled, just a little, then turned back to Tobey.

"Is this how you guys do it?" she asked. "Is that your act? You're kind of tough and quiet and he cracks the jokes?"

Again, Tobey was at a loss for words. It didn't help that he just couldn't stop staring at her.

But then a dark shadow appeared over them. The lights in the hall seemed to go dim. The cascading emerald mist lost its glow.

Suddenly Dino Brewster was there, injecting himself into the conversation.

"Hi, Julia," he said.

Tobey's heart plunged to his new shoes. Why in the world would these two know each other?

"Three million is way too much for this car, Dino," Julia told him directly.

"But that's what it costs," Dino replied. "Let's see what Ingram thinks."

"*I* am what Ingram thinks," she insisted. "And Ingram thinks it's worth two million at the most."

Dino shook his head. "Sorry, three million is the number."

"But three is absurd," she said. "And everyone here knows it. They loved the presentation—but why do you think nobody's bid on it yet?"

Dino didn't miss a beat. "There's still plenty of time for that. Plus, it's the best car I've driven since Indy—"

But then Pete interrupted again. He saw a wrong and had to right it. That's just the way he was.

"You've never driven this car," he told Dino dismissively. "Tobey has had the keys the whole time."

Julia smirked. "You want me to plug my ears and turn around while you guys get on the same page?"

Little Pete laughed at her joke. But Dino was staring daggers at him.

Still she continued her assault. "What's the top speed?" she asked Dino directly.

"One eighty," Dino replied—but Tobey answered at the same exact moment, except he said, "two thirty. . ."

She looked authentically surprised. "*Two hundred and thirty* miles per hour?"

Dino tried to explain. "He's talking about a theoretical top speed," he said, rather desperately.

She pointed to Tobey. "I know that he doesn't really talk much," she said. "But let's see if Mr. Strong and Silent can be less silent."

"She'll go two thirty," Tobey said simply.

"But the top NASCAR speed ever was two twenty-eight," she told him.

"This car is faster," Tobey replied calmly.

Finally she stopped talking for a moment. A wide smile lit up her face.

"Okay," she said, "eight o'clock tomorrow up in your neck of the woods at Shepperton. You get anything close to two thirty out of this car, Ingram will buy it on the spot."

Suddenly, Dino was excited again. "For three million?"

Julia giggled again. "Give or take a million," she said. "Mostly take."

With that, she walked away.

All three of them watched her go. But Dino was fuming.

"Two thirty," he growled at Tobey once she was out of earshot. "Are you crazy? What if I can't get the car up to that speed?"

"You can't," Tobey told him simply. "But I can. So I'll drive."

Dino could barely control his anger. While their collaboration to create the Super Shelby had been a success, mostly because Dino hadn't interfered with the building process, ever since the project had been completed, he'd been the same old Dino. Asshole, douche bag, tool.

As proof of this, in a low, threatening voice, he said to Tobey, "Don't even think about driving that car . . . and I mean, *ever.*"

Six

A GOOD EXAMPLE of just how affluent some residents of the Mount Kisco area were could be found about ten miles east of town.

It was called the Shepperton Motor Club, but essentially it was a private racetrack. While its owners were always quick to point out that it was more than just a place for the mega-rich to race their mega-expensive cars—that it was also a resort, a training ground, and a retreat—the truth was, in these things, size mattered. And Shepperton was nearly twice the size of the Mount Kisco country club, that rattrap closer to town.

In addition to all those other amenities, Shepperton boasted a 4.2-mile track that snaked its way through 175 acres of strategically placed woods, finely mowed lawns, and low grassy shoulders. It featured many grand corners, built with the great European tracks in mind, and had more than a mile and a half of straightaways, four hundred feet of elevation changes, and twenty-two turns, including three hairpins.

Membership there was ultra-exclusive; only about 1 percent of the 1 percent could get in, and the dues ran into the high six figures. Anyone owning what would be considered less than a typical supercar would be best off trying to get their kicks somewhere else.

This was why Tobey, despite his love for all things cars and racing, had never been past its gates. Until now.

The day had dawned bright and fiery, covering the private racetrack with bloodred colors. Tobey and Little Pete were the first to arrive. Passing through the security check as invited members of Dino Brewster, they drove slowly up the winding road leading to the main field.

"I've died and gone to heaven," Little Pete whispered on seeing the facilities, which included rows of well-maintained private garages, equipment buildings, and fuel houses. "I've always wondered what this place looked like up close."

"Me, too," Tobey sighed.

They rolled the Mustang off the flatbed truck, handling it with the utmost care. Once done, they both took a good look around.

"Where is everybody?" Pete asked, checking the time.

"I guess we're early," Tobey said.

He was glad for this—he wanted some time to think about what would come next.

He walked over to the Mustang and ran his hand along its roofline. He knew every inch of the supercar—every part, every gasket, every nut, screw, and bolt. The Super Mustang really *was* a work of art. He was proud of it, and proud of the Marshall team for doing such a great job.

Then he looked out onto the track. It was untouched so far for the day. Glistening. Inviting. Dewdrop perfect.

Little Pete knew Tobey well. He studied his friend as Tobey took turns admiring the car and then glancing out on the empty racetrack. Pete could almost hear the wheels spinning in Tobey's head. He knew what he was thinking.

"Tobey?" he said to him. "Tobey . . ."

But Tobey didn't reply.

So Little Pete walked up beside him and looked out on the track as well.

Then he said, "You've got to do it, bro."

Not a minute later, Tobey was behind the wheel of the Shelby Mustang, tearing around the racetrack.

He went through the first big turn at 180 mph—but that was just the beginning. He and his car were just warming up.

He shifted up to sixth gear, came out of the turn, and stomped on the accelerator. The speedometer began climbing.

. . . 190 . . . 200 . . . 210 . . .

A moment later he was rocketing down the first straightaway at an ungodly speed—exactly what the supercar had been designed to do.

Now it was up to him to prove his claims were true.

He went into the next turn high on the bank. That it cost him a few extra moments to take the longer line didn't bother him. This was all about building speed. Coming off the high bank, he would achieve a slingshot effect—or so he hoped. He needed all the velocity he could get so he could crank the Mustang up to the magic 230 mph on the next straightaway, before he ran out of road again.

Little Pete was standing alone back in the pits near the high turn. Tobey caught a glimpse of him in the microsecond it took to go by. He just barely saw that Pete had his hands up to his ears, trying to block out the noise of the Super Mustang's super engine.

That's a good sign, he thought.

Then Tobey hit the straightaway and put one eye on his speedometer.

It began to creep above 220 . . . 222 . . . 223 . . .

Back in the pits, Little Pete had taken his hands away from his ears, only to hear someone screaming. He turned to see Dino running toward him like a madman. He was pointing wildly at the Mustang as it rocketed around the next turn.

"*Stop him!*" Dino was screaming at Pete. "Goddammit! *Stop him!*"

Two minutes later, Tobey pulled into the pit area and climbed out of the Mustang. He was smiling broadly, a rarity.

But then Dino appeared, and the smile was gone.

"What *the fuck* are you doing, Marshall?" Dino screamed at him. "You don't own this car! You don't get to joyride in it!"

Tobey kept his cool. He just walked away from him.

"Top speed's a little over two thirty," he called over his shoulder to Dino. "We did it."

But Dino wasn't really listening. He grabbed Tobey, his fist reared back ready to punch him. But Tobey was much quicker. He caught Dino's arm and held it firm, making any punch impossible. Still, they were just seconds away from a major brawl.

Suddenly, a female voice rose above the fray.

"According to this . . ." the voice said.

It was enough to freeze Dino and Tobey in place. They looked up to see Julia, as beautiful as ever, holding up a radar gun.

"According to this," she said again, "it's true . . . Tobey hit two thirty . . ."

A man in an expensive suit was standing next to her. He had binoculars around his neck.

He was Mark Ingram, filthy rich, playboy-ish, a ranking member at Shepperton, and the owner of many high-performance cars.

"That was some driving, son," Ingram said to Tobey. "And that's one hell of a car."

He looked at the Super Mustang again and then back at the small group in the pits.

"And it's gonna cost me three million?" he asked.

Dino looked over at Julia and then back at Ingram.

"Yes, sir," Dino said. "It is."

"Two point seven . . ." Julia piped up.

Dino looked back at her with dark eyes. But she had no problem staring him down.

Ingram broke the stalemate. "If Julia says it's worth two point seven," he said. "I'll pay two point seven . . . take it or leave it."

It was official just a few minutes later.

Ingram wrote Dino a check for $2.7 million without blinking an eye. Then, to celebrate his purchase, he put on a racing helmet, got behind the wheel of the Mustang and roared away.

This should have been a special moment for all involved, but Dino ruined that. He was still ready to kill Tobey.

"What *the hell* were you thinking?" he half screamed at him again. "If you had wrecked that car—or blown the engine, or anything, this whole deal would have been fucked."

Tobey remained cool. "But none of that happened," he replied casually. "And we sold the car, didn't we? I thought that was the whole point."

But then Little Pete butted in. "You never could have gotten that car to two thirty. Even on a track. Only Tobey could do that—and that's why the guy bought it."

But Dino was still glaring at Tobey. This wasn't about money. This was about ego—and Dino's was supersized.

"You think you're a better driver than me, Marshall?" he hissed at Tobey.

But before Tobey could reply, Little Pete butted in again.

"I *know* he's a better driver than you," he told Dino.

Dino suddenly turned on Little Pete.

"You know, I'm about done with you," he said angrily, taking a step in Pete's direction.

Tobey was immediately in Dino's face.

"Back off, Dino," he warned him.

But Dino would not relent. He was fuming.

"I'll beat you on a road," he seethed at Tobey. "On a track, on the dirt, or anywhere else you want to race. You name it, Marshall."

But Little Pete laughed in Dino's face.

"Last time I checked," he said, "Tobey beat you every time you raced in high school."

"Well, a lot's happened since high school, little man," Dino spit back at him.

Little Pete straightened himself up to his full diminutive height—but Tobey interceded once again. He was trying hard to play peacemaker.

"You're the man," he told Dino. "You're the pro. Okay? You got nothing to prove to me. Let's just move on."

But Dino was just not buying it. The veins in his head looked like they were all going to pop.

"No," he said. "Let's race. If you win, I give you my seventy-five-percent cut of the Mustang deal. You lose, you give me your twenty-five percent."

Tobey froze. The prospect of such big money gave him pause—and stopped him from thinking clearly, at least for the moment. He couldn't help it—$2.7 million? That kind of money could change everything for him.

"Well," he said, "that would make it interesting."

Before he could say another word, Dino told him, "I'll pick you guys up at your shop, four o'clock . . . Just be ready."

With that, Dino stormed away.

But Tobey was confused.

"What are we racing?" he called after Dino. "And where?"

But Dino never replied.

Seven

▋▋▋▋▋▋▋▋▋▋▋▋▋▋▋▋▋▋▋▋▋▋▋

THE MOST EXPENSIVE house inside the Mount Kisco city limits was an enormous Tudor-style mansion located in an east side gated community known as Guard Hill.

It was late afternoon when the black Mercedes sedan sped past this mansion's wrought iron gates and roared up the long driveway that led to the grand home.

No sooner had the Mercedes stopped at the front door than Little Pete excitedly jumped out of the backseat. Dino and Tobey climbed out of the front seats with somewhat less enthusiasm and joined him.

"That's the biggest house I've ever seen," Little Pete exclaimed.

"It's my uncle's place," Dino said. "He's in Monaco or someplace."

Tobey and Pete continued to gape at the mansion. As with the Shepperton Motor Club, they had heard of this place, but had never gotten any closer to it than driving by its front gate.

Dino noted their fascination and was ready to take advantage of it. He put on a pair of leather driving gloves he'd taken from his pocket, then pushed them along.

"C'mon," he told them. "I want to show you something."

Dino had been virtually silent since picking them up; Tobey didn't know what he was up to, exactly. They followed him around the side of the mansion and up to a pristine parking garage. It was almost as impressive as the main house.

"Get ready to piss your pants," Dino told them. He dramatically pushed a button on the side of the building, and three garage doors opened automatically.

Inside, sitting in separate bays, were three of the most fantastic cars Tobey had ever seen.

They were Koenigsegg Ageras. Designed and built in Sweden, they were aptly known as "hypercars." Ultra sleek and very low to the ground, they looked like they'd been conceived by someone one hundred years in the future, or perhaps an ET. A wealthy ET. Extremely rare and extremely expensive, their tires alone cost tens of thousands of dollars. With modifications, a complete racing car could run more than $4 million.

The mansion was past history to Tobey and Little Pete

now. They had only heard of these incredible cars, and seen photographs. To be in their presence was almost overwhelming.

"These aren't even legal in the United States," Dino told them. "They've got no registration, no plates—so technically, they don't exist."

Tobey didn't want to believe what he thought was happening.

"Why are you showing these to us?" he asked Dino. "Just to prove your family has money?"

Dino just laughed at him. "No, you hick," he said. "This is what we're going to race in. Winner takes the two point seven million."

"And there's three of them," Pete said, still awestruck.

"This is what the real pros drive," Dino went on. "Zero to one twenty in eight seconds. Top speed—well, who knows? Are you afraid of that much power, Marshall?"

Pete laughed at the comment. "But Dino," he said. "I thought you didn't go faster than one eighty?"

Dino finally snapped. He grabbed Little Pete by the jacket and roughly pulled him over.

"You got a big mouth for someone who's just a fan," he growled at Pete.

"Then let me race," Pete spit right back at him.

Once again, Tobey had to step in. He pulled the two combatants apart.

"Okay, happy to have you, Petey," Dino said. "Like you said, we've got three cars. So one of them is for you."

Little Pete couldn't believe it. "Awesome!" he shouted. "I'm in."

But Tobey didn't like this. These cars were way out of their league, Dino included. And while he knew he'd have to go up against his rival, if not for the $2.7 million, then only to shut him up, involving Pete in the race sounded a little too dangerous.

"It's better if you sit this one out," Tobey told his friend. "The other guys would never believe you did it anyway."

But Dino laughed darkly. "Let him be a big boy, to match his big mouth," he told Tobey, pointing to the three cars. "We've got three identical Ageras. It's an even playing field. So, let's do it."

Tobey was still trying to process just what kind of insanity was taking place. He'd had no idea this was what Dino had in mind.

Dino held out a hat. It contained three sets of keys.

"Finish line is the end of the bridge over Route 684," he told them. "It should be lit up by the time we get there."

Little Pete reached into the hat and pulled out a key. Dino drew next, then Tobey.

Pete excitedly pointed his key toward the Koenigseggs and the one on the end lit up. He hustled over to it; Tobey was right on his heels.

He said to Pete, "Listen to me . . . Don't mess with him. Let me race him. You stay out of it and just go for a nice ride."

But Pete just shook his head.

"Relax, Tobey," he said. "You know I'm a good driver. I got this."

But Tobey was still concerned for his friend.

"You've got to go easy," he warned him. "Your Camaro has what—480 horse? This thing has like 950 . . ."

Dino interrupted.

"More like 1140 . . ." he said.

Tobey shook his head again. Even though the idea of racing a car with that much horsepower excited him to no end, he was getting a bad feeling about this.

But then Pete turned back to him.

"This is my vision, bro," he said. "This is how I saw you winning the De Leon. You beat Dino. You take his car and win. Plus, if we both beat him, he'll have to move out of the country or something . . ."

Tobey smiled. He really loved his "little brother." And it was hard to argue with him.

"Okay, but just play it smart," he told Pete.

Pete gave him a thumbs-up and then jumped into the hypercar.

"Time to rock and roll!" he yelled.

The intersection of Routes 76 and 184 was about a mile outside downtown Mount Kisco. It was the crossing of two little-used roads and one of many approaches the locals could use to get on Interstate 684.

It was late afternoon now and quiet. A car was stopped

at the intersection, waiting for the light to change. Meanwhile another car was approaching from Route 184, traveling in the slow lane.

Suddenly a loud roar shattered the peaceful scene. A second later Dino's Koenigsegg appeared out of nowhere. It squealed into the intersection, causing a storm of dust and exhaust, violently drifting sideways and perfectly splitting the two civilian cars.

His sudden appearance caused one of the civilian cars to nearly clip his rear end. At the same moment, and for the same reason, the second car slammed into the first, spinning it like a child's top and throwing it onto the median.

Dino was able to avoid being caught up in the collision. He regained control of the Koenigsegg hypercar and pushed his accelerator to the floor. His engine screaming, he rocketed away with just minimal damage to his left rear taillight.

A split second later, Little Pete roared into the intersection. Seeing the melee Dino had caused, he was forced to drift way out to avoid colliding with the two hapless civilian cars. His maneuver successful, he took off after Dino.

Both Koenigseggs now accelerated to 130 mph and roared through a bending stretch of roadway with lakes on either side.

Pete was barely able to contain himself. He was pressing the gas harder and harder, all the while shouting at the top of his lungs. He'd never driven anything even close to the Koenigsegg. For him, this was something from one of his visions.

They flew by a civilian car doing the 55 mph speed limit. It was as if it was standing still. Pete zoomed right up on Dino's bumper and was enjoying every second of it. Tobey was following close behind. He'd fallen back intentionally so he could keep his eyes on Little Pete. As a result, he still had some ground to make up. But at the same time, he was only a few seconds behind both of them.

His eyes were glued on Little Pete as the three hyper-cars approached a turn. He saw his friend go wide, so Tobey started his own turn early, sliding inside, half on, half off the roadway's shoulder. Accelerating at exactly the right moment, Tobey came out of the turn just a little ahead of Pete, putting him just five car lengths behind Dino.

The three hypercars were now on a long, rolling part of the roadway, passing civilian vehicles like they were frozen in place. Zooming inside and outside, on the shoulder one moment, skirting the median the next, the trio of Koenigseggs were now doing 180 mph.

Suddenly, up ahead, a Chevy pickup truck came into view. Its elderly driver was barely going the speed limit, and was listening to his radio at high volume.

But when he glanced into his rearview mirror, he did a double take. An instant later, Dino's Koenigsegg blew past him.

The driver couldn't believe his eyes. The hypercar went by him in a flash. He looked at his own speed—just under

65 mph. When he looked up again, Tobey and Pete had roared by him as well.

The three hypercars entered a dead straightaway. Dino was still in the lead, but Tobey was right behind him, with Little Pete right on Tobey's bumper.

They flew over a crown in the highway, each Koenigsegg going airborne for a moment before coming back to earth. In front of them now, just a quarter mile away, was another intersection. At that moment, a large truck, pulling a horse trailer, was crossing through.

The three Koenigseggs were traveling in excess of 200 mph now. At that speed, all three would hit the truck in five seconds.

The truck driver saw them coming. Not quite believing what was happening, he panicked and slammed on the brakes, blocking the intersection

Dino was the first to hit his own brakes, his Koenigsegg fishtailing wildly from side to side. Tobey saw Dino's brake lights and reacted instantly. But he didn't hit his brakes. Rather, he laid on the accelerator and made an aggressive move around the truck. The maneuver avoided a collision, but an instant later, he found himself on the other side of the highway's median, going the wrong way, and heading right into oncoming traffic.

Meanwhile, Dino was trying to get around the back end of the horse trailer, but Little Pete was too close on his tail. They made their move at the same time, Dino's nose almost clipping Little Pete's rear end. Little Pete reacted immediately, swerving wide. He avoided colliding with Dino, but he was suddenly sent spinning onto the grass.

For that one long moment, Pete came very close to losing it. But with another sharp turn of the wheel and a boot of the gas, he was quickly back on the pavement and running straight again.

All this bizarre high-speed maneuvering had put Tobey in the lead—the only problem being he was traveling on the wrong side of the highway. He was madly weaving back and forth, getting out of the way of oncoming trucks, cars, and vans, all while still going nearly 200 mph.

All the while, he was desperately searching for an opening in the median, a spot where he could get back on the right side of the road. But the median strip was lined with trees, rocks, and bushes—and no openings. He had no choice but to press on in the wrong direction.

Over on the right side of the road, and with very little traffic ahead of them, Dino and Little Pete had accelerated up to 210 mph. This allowed both cars to gain serious ground on Tobey. Realizing what was happening, Tobey buried his gas pedal as well. But then he saw another car coming straight at him.

The driver swerved before Tobey could, crashing over the median strip. Immediately losing control in the high grass, the civilian slid through a clump of trees . . . and right into the path of Dino and Little Pete.

Luckily, their instincts took over. Little Pete swerved inside the careening car while Dino went to the outside.

It was close, but their driving skills got them by the hapless driver in a flash.

Tobey was watching all this from the other side of the highway. Finally, he spotted an opening in the median strip ahead. With a quick jerk of his steering wheel, he slid through the gap and was suddenly back on the right side of the road.

But another civilian car that had swerved to avoid Tobey was now right in Little Pete's path. Little Pete went left and got around the car, but then it moved over and went right into Dino's path. Dino hit his brakes again, swerving wildly to the right. He avoided a collision, but when the smoke cleared, he found himself in last place, looking at the butt ends of Tobey's and Little Pete's hypercars.

The three Koenigseggs roared up to another intersection. This one was clear. With incredible precision, all three drifted onto Freedom Parkway. They were now in the final stretch of their race.

The parkway was conveniently devoid of traffic. Up ahead, all three drivers could see a bridge all lit up.

They were roaring along now at their fastest speeds yet. Tobey was in front, Little Pete right on his bumper, with Dino riding Pete's bumper in turn. Maintaining this tight bunch, all three accelerated to an incredible 250 mph.

Little Pete looked up to his rearview mirror to see Dino drafting off him. This told him Dino was about to make one last desperate move before the race was over and he lost $2 million. But Pete was ready for him.

The bridge was right up ahead, and their speed was now more than 260 mph. Suddenly Dino made his move, trying to pass Little Pete on the outside.

But it was not a clean maneuver—and Dino violently clipped the back of Little Pete's car.

Suddenly Little Pete was airborne, and not by a few inches. All four of his tires left the ground, hurtling him ten feet above the pavement.

Still moving at tremendous speed, Pete landed hard, hitting the bridge's concrete foundation nose first. The impact caused the hypercar to begin a series of sickening cartwheels. Pete tumbled over and over, smashing through a light pole, and then against a cement barrier. The multimillion dollar car was disintegrating with each bounce, leaving a cloud of glass, metal, and rubber behind.

Tobey saw it all. Looking through his rearview mirror, he saw Pete's car, now in flames, careen off a bridge support, go clear over the railing, and disappear below.

Tobey stood on his brakes. Spinning the steering wheel at the same time, he turned 180 degrees in an instant. He was just seconds from winning the brutal $2.7 million race—but suddenly all thoughts of the money were gone. He went back for Little Pete instead.

As he did so, Dino blew right past him and crossed the other end of the bridge, winning the race.

Tobey was at the crash site in seconds. He jumped out of the Koenigsegg and slid down the hundred-foot embankment to the edge of the river.

Little Pete's car was there, but it was barely recognizable. It was upside down and being consumed by flames, its four wheels swaying as if suffering from compound fractures.

Tobey could see Little Pete inside, his lifeless body just barely visible through the fire. He tried to reach inside to grab him, but the heat was too intense. He whipped off his jacket, putting it up to shield his face and hands, and tried again—and again. And again.

"Pete!" Tobey screamed from the depths of his soul. "Jesus . . . Pete!"

But it was no good.

The flames were just too much.

The next thing Tobey knew, he was surrounded by flashing lights coming from the bridge above. The sound of sirens filled his ears. There were police and firefighters everywhere.

Little Pete's body was in front of him, covered with a tarp. Some EMTs and the coroner were struggling to move it over the rocks and up the embankment.

Another EMT was beside Tobey, trying to treat his burns, but Tobey was numb all over.

He could only stare out at the river and watch the water go by.

Eight

FIVE DAYS LATER

INSIDE A SMALL graveyard on the west side of Mount Kisco, a group of people all dressed in black were gathered around a freshly dug grave.

A priest's words drifted above the sad scene.

"Fear not," he intoned, "for I am with you. Be not dismayed, for I am your God. I will strengthen you. Yes, I will help you, I will uphold you with my righteous right hand."

Most everyone in the crowd was crying or fighting off tears. But Anita was particularly distraught. Her younger brother, Pete, was now deceased and about to be lowered into the ground.

For comfort in this difficult hour, she was leaning on the shoulder of another mourner—Dino Brewster.

"Behold," the priest went on, "all those who were incensed against you shall be ashamed and disgraced. They shall be nothing. You shall seek them and not find them—those who contended with you. Those who war against you shall be as nothing. For I will hold your right hand, saying to you, 'Fear not. I will help you.'"

Benny and Joe Peck were also there. Benny was taking it very hard. When the priest finished the final prayer, Benny shut his eyes and tried to breathe deep, but it didn't help. Nothing helped. His friend was gone.

Joe, on the other hand, was staring right across the open grave, leveling his eyes on Dino.

It was an icy glare, chilling to the bone. And to Joe, the fact that Dino refused to look back at him said it all.

Nine

THE INTERROGATION ROOM was cold and dank. The walls were plain, dull green, with old paint chipping off just about everywhere. Everything smelled of spilled coffee, cigarette smoke, and sweat.

Tobey was sitting in a squeaky metal chair, an old wooden desk in front of him. It seemed like he'd been inside the damp, smelly room for days. He couldn't really tell. Time as he knew it had lost all meaning for him.

His entire world had changed the moment Little Pete died. It was like he was walking and talking and existing by some kind of weird remote control. Whenever he closed his eyes all he could see was Pete burning to death in the crashed hypercar. The flames, the smoke, the noise, the river water rushing by. Tobey knew nothing would ever be the same.

But the real blow came later on that awful day. That's when the police charged *him* with killing Little Pete.

Two state police detectives were sitting across the table from him now. They'd been questioning him for hours, days—again, Tobey really didn't know. He was just numb, inside and out.

"Okay, let's go through this one more time, Mr. Marshall," one of the detectives started again. "The report still shows this fatality was caused by a two-car accident."

The second detective piped up.

"Tell us again where you claim this mysterious third vehicle was," he said.

Tobey began speaking again—but it sounded like someone else's voice. He'd told them the exact same story more than a dozen times already.

"My car was about two lengths out in front," he said wearily, pointing to a diagram of the accident scene sitting on the old wooden table. "Pete was there. Dino Brewster was right behind him. Dino hit Pete's back bumper hard and at an angle—and Pete lost control of his car. That's how it happened. Dino caused the crash."

The detectives shook their heads. "But Dino has two solid witnesses," one said. "And they both say they were with him all day and the whole night. So there's no way he could have been there to cause that crash."

But again the detectives' words were barely registering with Tobey. Try as he might, he couldn't think clearly about anything else—except the fact that Little Pete was gone.

The cops were relentless, though. They took his lack of feeling as a sign of weakness—and a symptom that he was lying about what had really happened on the bridge.

"The owner of Brewster Motors reported *two* Koenigseggs were stolen last week," the other detective said harshly. "That's two cars, not three. His report also says those two cars were stolen seven minutes before police arrived at the scene of the crash."

Tobey momentarily snapped out of his stupor.

"The owner of Brewster Motors is Dino's uncle," he told the cops. "He's lying. They're *all* lying. Dino did it. Dino was there."

"You're the only one who places Dino at the scene," the detective replied. "You got any other 'facts' you'd like to share?"

"There were three cars," Tobey insisted wearily. "Dino was there . . ."

The detectives exchanged glances. People lied to them every day; they were used to it, and in their own way, numb to it. They simply weren't buying Tobey's story.

"Then where's the third car?" one of them asked. "Wouldn't it be wrecked, too?"

At that point, Tobey went back into his disembodied state.

"This isn't happening," he said to himself over and over. "This just isn't happening . . ."

* * *

The trial was a nightmare.

Tobey vowed early on just to tell the story straight, as it happened, blow by blow. And that's what he did, over and over, during endless hours of cross-examination.

But he was up against the powerful Brewster family, and they proved to be a formidable foe. No matter how many times he told the truth, the prosecutors put on rebuttal witnesses, all of whom were either in the Brewster family's employ or were friends of theirs. These people lied under oath that Dino was nowhere near the scene of the accident, and that only two Koenigseggs could have been "stolen" that night because only two Koenigseggs were in the mansion's garage in the first place.

The third hypercar, the one Dino had been driving, had vanished. Tobey's lawyer tried to find documentation on its sale, its purchase price, and when it arrived in the United States, but failed on all three accounts. The only evidence available was on the purchase of two Koenigseggs by Dino's wealthy uncle. There was plenty of documentation for them: routing slips, delivery confirmations, shipping manifests.

Aided by all this, and the implication that the Brewsters were an upstanding family while Tobey was just a hard-edged grease monkey, the prosecutors were able to make the case that there were only two Koenigseggs in the garage that afternoon, that there were only two racing on that road, and that Little Pete's car had been forced off the road, which led to his death. And the only one around who could have done it was Tobey.

The charge was vehicular manslaughter plus auto theft.

At one point, Tobey's attorney negotiated a deal where if Tobey pled guilty, he would get the charges reduced, and thus get a lighter sentence. But Tobey refused. He was innocent, and there was no way he was going to plead guilty to killing his best friend when he didn't do it.

The crew from the garage showed up at the trial every day. Before every court session Tobey scanned the gallery and always found Benny, Joe Peck, and Finn sitting there in their bad suits and ill-fitting ties, giving him the thumbs-up and offering signs of encouragement. But even their moral support couldn't change the inevitable.

In all it only took three weeks. Tobey was found guilty on both counts and sentenced to two to five years in state prison.

It was devastating to hear the verdict read aloud. But it only got worse after that. Tobey had spent so much money on the trial that he couldn't afford any kind of appeal. He'd sold his family's house, some family heirlooms, even his Gran Torino. But it was all for nothing.

The day he walked into prison, he was broke, he was a convicted felon, and his father's business had been shut down.

The destruction of his life as he knew it was complete.

He'd lost everything.

Part
Four

Ten

TOBEY'S FIRST FEW days in prison were pure hell.

The loneliest sound he'd ever heard was the clank of the huge steel door shutting behind him the moment he walked inside.

Good-bye world, he thought. *Maybe forever.*

He'd tried to psych himself up in the days and hours leading up to it. Tried to tell himself he'd be strong and that he could get through it—but he quickly realized nothing could prepare him for the nightmare he'd found himself in.

From when they took his clothes, to his delousing—or "douching," as it was known—to putting on his gray prison uniform, to when they finally put him in his cell and locked the door, none of it seemed real, and he just couldn't get over the feeling that it was actually happening to someone else.

Then there were the chains.

No matter where he was those first few days, or what time, day or night, all he could hear were chains. Chain shackles dragging on the floor. Guards carrying chains to bind someone up. Other prisoners with chains hidden in their pants, to be used as weapons, on their way to give some "new meat" a beat down—or worse.

Chains . . . He even began to hear them in his sleep.

It took a few days for the cold reality of it all to sink in. The realization that his life was no longer his own. He was not allowed to do anything unless he was told to. Eat, sleep, shit, shave. Even flicking his cell's light switch on or off was forbidden.

Everything was regimented; everything was done their way. The lights came on at 5:00 a.m. Every prisoner had to be ready to leave his cell precisely five minutes later. A long, slow march down to the cafeteria followed, more chains dragging everywhere. Breakfast was usually tepid oatmeal or cold processed eggs. Each was equally bad.

Back to the cells for the mandatory count and, more often than not, a surprise search. New meat were always harassed by the guards. Getting one's cell tossed could be a daily or even hourly event.

Some kind of workday followed. Tobey had been assigned to the laundry. It was hot, smelly, disgusting duty, a place where the fouled sheets, towels, uniforms, socks, and underwear of 2,500 inmates was never-ending.

The only break was the long march down to lunch, which was just as awful as breakfast. Then more hot and sweaty work, until dinner, which was usually the worst meal of all.

Lights went out at 8:00 p.m., followed by a night of ear-piercing screams, demonic laughter, repulsive grunting—and more chains. Then, it started all over again at 5:00 a.m. the next day.

The idea was to take away every last bit of a person's physical freedom. And Tobey knew early on that once that was complete, his freedom to think would be taken next.

The prison was also an extremely dangerous place, as he soon found out. The guards weren't there to protect the inmates. It was clear from the beginning that was not how the System worked. The guards were more like onlookers, referees. Caretakers of the status quo. Many of them were corrupt, paid off by the prisoners or their families. Their main concern, then, was that no one on the inside rocked the boat.

The System itself was run by the Lifers—gangs of murderers and rapists who had nothing to lose by beating and robbing new meat. Sadistic and psychotic, they pretty much had full run of the place, including access to anyone's cell or work area. An attack could come at anytime and in any place.

Most perverse was that this constant terror provided

a kind of horrific stability to the place. Management through fear ruled within the prison walls—not guards, or guns, or billy clubs. Just plain, unadulterated fear.

And the newer you were to the System, the more dangerous it could be.

On his fifth day in, Tobey was washing his face in the shitter when he looked in the mirror to see another prisoner, a gang member, standing behind him, holding a machete.

He was giving Tobey the finger-across-his-throat sign. The meaning was clear: You're next.

Later that day, another inmate came up to Tobey in the laundry and claimed he'd seen what had happened earlier. He offered to help Tobey out of the jam in return for some unspecified services Tobey could provide him in the future.

Tobey was smart enough to know he was being set up. Much to the man's surprise, he told the helpful inmate no thanks; he'd handle the situation himself.

The man replied, "Okay—nice knowing you."

Later that night, Tobey heard the door to his cell open. It was supposed to be locked at 8:00 p.m., but obviously this was not a guard coming in to check on him.

Tobey was ready with the only weapon he had at his disposal: a sharpened pencil. He saw the glint of the machete drawing near and was never more scared in his life. But that's when his survival instincts kicked in.

He aimed low and stuck his would-be assailant in the groin with the pencil. It went in deep and as smoothly as a knife through butter. The attacker doubled over from the unexpected preemptive strike, hitting the floor of the cell hard and conveniently cracking open his skull.

When the guards eventually arrived, they found the attacker curled up on the ground, bleeding profusely, with Tobey sitting calmly on the edge of his bunk.

When they asked what happened, Tobey told them, "He tripped."

He knew what would happen next. Though he was sure he'd gained some cred among those lowly prisoners who lived in daily fear of the System, he also knew he'd be a marked man by the Lifers.

The next day at breakfast, he walked up to the largest member of the machete man's gang and, without warning, started wailing on him with his fists and feet. To Tobey's good fortune, the man's weapon of choice, a doorknob carried in a sock, fell out of his pocket. Tobey picked it up and started thrashing him with that as well. The others in the machete gang stood back and let it happen. That was the way these things worked. It took Tobey two long minutes to hammer his victim into unconsciousness.

When the guards arrived and saw what had happened, they were convinced Tobey was not someone who wanted to play within the System. He was immediately put in shackles and put in the Hole, prison slang for solitary confinement.

This was not like his cell, with bars and walls and a

window. This was a stark concrete room, just five feet by eight feet. There was no bunk; just a metal slab. There was no toilet; just an open drain in the floor. There was no window; just three vertical slits in the door, and a slot at the bottom for meal trays.

There would be no reading material, no music, no pens, or paper, or photographs to hang or look at. There was nothing but the walls, the drain, and the metal slab.

When they closed the door on him, the guard said, "See you in six months."

After that, Tobey sat in the corner and shook uncontrollably for hours. But he'd accomplished his goal. He was alone—with no one to bother him.

From that day on, he began preparing for what he hoped would be the second part of his life.

He also came up with a plan.

Tobey was not a religious person. He'd never gone to church, never followed any one creed. So, he didn't know any prayers, other than the ordinary generic ones.

That didn't matter. For this, the longest two years of his life, in jail for killing his best friend, knowing full well he was innocent and that the guilty party was not just out there walking free but also banging his ex-girlfriend . . .

For this, an ordinary prayer would not do.

For this, he needed to make up one of his own.

His meals arrived like clockwork every day. Pushed through the slot at the bottom of his door, they came with plastic utensils, all of which had to be accounted for when the tray was taken away.

One day Tobey broke one of the plastic knives in half and stuck the handle into a mash of leftover food. He was hoping no one would bother to check if the other half was still attached. He waited a week, but no one said a word.

He used this half of knife to painstakingly carve his prayer into the concrete wall, chip by chip, in a space right above the door. That way he could see it, read it anytime he wanted, and yet it would be invisible to the guards looking in on him.

He wrote his prayer just two or three words at a time, and only after much thought went into what would fit and what would not. Each word had to be perfect, because there was no chance for erasure. The concrete was unforgiving in that respect. Once he carved his letters into it, they were there to stay.

It took him more than two months to complete it, but in the end he was happy with it. In his mind, it *was* perfect; it said it all.

They took everything from me.
But I do not fear, for you are with me.
All those who defied me
Shall be ashamed and disgraced.
Those who wage war against me
Shall perish.
I will find strength, find guidance
And I will triumph.

He recited the prayer at least a couple dozen times a day.

On some days, even more.

He spent his time in isolation doing a regimen of his own.

Morning was devoted to push-ups, leg squats, and other kinds of exercise, including many isometric drills he'd made up.

He'd been scrappy and fearless when he first went into prison. By the end of his first two months, he still had his lean frame, but whatever body fat he'd accumulated by drinking beer and eating junk food on the outside had been replaced by pure, solid muscle.

But he knew he would need more than just six-pack abs if his long-range plan were to succeed. So afternoons were reserved for doing mind exercises of a very specific order.

He would sit in his corner and put himself into a kind of trance and relive every car race he'd ever been in. From go-carts to shifter cars to his first street races. Every box race he'd driven in; every pull race he'd run out on I-684. Even that last fateful one with Dino and Little Pete—he was able to conjure them up vividly and replay them again, over and over in his head.

He was able to recall every move he'd made, commit to memory every positive maneuver, and dwell especially on the ones that turned out to be wrong. He reviewed in his mind every part, gear, paddle, and switch of every vehicle he'd ever raced, from the shifter cars on, concentrating, of course, on his beloved Gran Torino.

He was able to immerse himself in his memories, which were all he really had left. But he was able to learn from them—and that was the most important thing.

On special nights, and he did this sparingly, he would put himself into his trance and think about those few glorious moments he'd experienced that morning driving the Shelby Mustang at Shepperton. He always began this particular mind exercise by remembering everything exactly how it was that day. The weather, how the track looked. How Little Pete was so excited. How he brought the Shelby into that first turn wide so he could slingshot himself onto the straightaway. How he had reached and then surpassed that magic 230 mph number.

After many of those special sessions he would fall asleep sitting upright in his corner and dream about that special morning all over again.

Those hours, days, and months in the Hole strengthened him physically, but more important, they bulked him up mentally.

He knew that would be needed most of all for what lay ahead.

He spent a total of thirteen months in the Hole, extended by his mouthing off to his guards at one point, and when he was caught, by design, stealing his plastic utensils.

When he was finally let out into the general population, he fell in with a bunch of fellow motorheads. Car thieves, mostly, they formed a substantial group and were pretty much left alone by the other gangs.

Just one day out of the Hole, he got a prison tattoo. It was simple. Written on his left forearm, it read: "Pete 392." His intention was to always have something there to remind him of his little brother, his friend.

It was only later that he realized that, by extension, anytime he looked at it, it also reminded him of Pete's beautiful sister, Anita.

Then came that day, exactly one month before his release, when he got the letter from Benny, talking about that year's De Leon—and how Monarch was looking for racers.

At that moment, Tobey knew it had all been worth it. Because suddenly, he was sure about what he'd been working for.

No one ever came to visit him while he was in prison. That's the way he'd wanted it. He didn't write any letters during the majority of his incarceration, either. Phone calls to Benny and Joe Peck had gotten him by.

But the one letter he did write had been to Mark Ingram, the wealthy owner of the Super Shelby Mustang.

Tobey had started that letter out with the words, "You will think this is a strange request, but . . ."

After that, the letters went back and forth furiously with Joe and Benny. The phone calls became more frequent, too. Something was building. His plan was moving full speed ahead.

When his last day finally came, Tobey didn't even read the prison release papers. He simply signed on the dotted line and pushed them back under the metal mesh window to the prison employee.

He looked different. Older, rougher—tougher. But he felt different, too. No more wasting time. No more whining about the bum deal he'd gotten.

He had important things to do.

He picked up the bag holding his meager belongings and waited for the last barred door to open.

Then he walked out into the sunlight and tasted freedom for the first time in two years.

Just outside the release gate, an old Ford pickup truck was waiting. Benny was behind the wheel.

He leapt out of the cab as soon as Tobey walked out. He gave Tobey a quick pound-hug, then they both jumped into the truck.

"Where's Joe?" Tobey asked Benny simply.

"Already on the road with the Beast," Benny reported. "If your plan is going to work, he's going to need that head start."

"What about Finn?" Tobey asked.

Benny shook his head. "We still haven't convinced him," he replied. "He went down another path. But we're still trying."

Benny turned the ignition key and started the old truck.

"But has the car come through?" Benny asked his friend. "That's the most important thing."

Tobey checked his watch. "We'll know in an hour."

"Okay," Benny said. "But we're cutting it a little close, don't you think?"

Tobey just shrugged and looked out the window, his thoughts already a million miles away.

"Hey, Tobey," Benny said, bringing him back to reality.

Tobey turned to his friend.

"Good to see you out, man," Benny told him.

Tobey just nodded, and almost smiled.

It was good to be out.

Eleven

▬▬▬▬▬▬▬

TOBEY AND BENNY reached their destination about an hour later.

It was an abandoned building located at 6565 Main Street, Mount Kisco.

Many of its windows had been broken and its doors busted in. Junk cars sat deteriorating in the parking lot; litter and trash were everywhere. The sign that once proudly read, "Marshall Motors Est. 1974" was hanging half off and had turned to rust.

The old garage. The place where he'd grown up. The place that had so many memories. It was gut-wrenching for Tobey to see it like this.

And it got worse. Wrapped around the garage's front door was a stream of yellow tape festooned with orange stickers from the sheriff's department announcing the property had been put in foreclosure. For Tobey, this was just adding insult to injury.

He and Benny climbed out of the Ford pickup. They examined the thick chain that was keeping the garage's front door shut. The door's glass itself was dirty and smeared, the numerals "6565" barely readable anymore.

It was a sad moment for both of them.

"I heard they're turning it into a Jack in the Box," Benny told him. "Just what Mount Kisco needs. More junk food."

Tobey tried to stay emotionless, but it was hard to do.

"I'm just glad my old man isn't alive to see this," he said. "It would have broken his heart."

Tobey took a long look around, checking for cops. Certain the coast was clear, he kicked a small hole in the glass door. Wrapping his fist in his jacket, he kept punching the hole until it was big enough for them to squeeze through.

He was the first to step inside. He had to take it in slowly. This place—once jumping with business, the sound of tools working, paint being sprayed, always with either loud rap music playing over the bedlam or Monarch's voice booming—now it was quiet and dark and a mess. This place that had been so special to him—first, working with his father, learning the trade, and then their utter triumph in building the Mustang—now . . . it was a place of vandalism. Thieves had broken in and stolen all the tools. The paint room was riddled with graffiti. Even the car lifts were gone. The inside looked even worse than the outside.

The photos that had been hanging on the wall had all

fallen, their glass frames cracked or shattered completely. Some of the pictures had turned yellow and wrinkled. Others were gone altogether.

This was a snapshot of failure. Tobey had promised his father that he would keep the garage open, no matter what. Now it was like something found in a ghost town— a thing of the past.

So what about the future? Tobey thought, giving the place another long, sad look. Would it be better? *Could* it be better?

He'd psyched himself up so much in prison, dreaming yet another dream, that he had been sky high. But looking at the dilapidated garage and how it had turned out, he suddenly wondered if he'd just been fooling himself all along. Would his grand plan be possible to pull off?

His answer came a second later.

There was a sudden, loud noise outside. The roar of a huge engine, the screeching of big tires—sounds that had not been heard anywhere near the Marshall Motors building in a long time.

A car had pulled into the parking lot. Silver ghost finish. Big wheels. Extremely sleek and sexy. A wave of smoke from its exhaust reached Tobey's nostrils, and he recognized it right away.

Only a little more than two years had gone by—but it might as well have been a lifetime.

It was the Mustang. The Shelby-designed supercar that they'd built here and sold to Ingram what seemed like a century ago.

It was like seeing an old friend; one you never thought you'd see ever again.

Then the Mustang's door opened, and an extremely attractive female stepped out. She was dressed in a way that would have made a supermodel jealous. Short, tight dress. High heels. Dramatic hair. Of all that had already happened to Tobey that day, this stunned him the most. He knew her, but he hadn't really thought about her, not until this moment. In fact, he'd almost forgotten just how beautiful she was.

It was not Anita, though.

It was Julia.

Suddenly it wasn't so dark and dreary around the Marshall Motors building.

But while he'd been expecting the car, he definitely hadn't been expecting her.

They met just outside the broken door. She smelled as good as she looked—but Tobey had to stay cool.

"Thanks for the delivery," he told her. "And thank Ingram for me. We won't let him down."

Then Tobey called over his shoulder to Benny, "What do you think? First American car to win the De Leon?"

Benny laughed. "Well, that's your big plan, isn't it? That's why Ingram loaned you his car."

Tobey held out his hand, expecting Julia to pass him the keys. But she didn't.

"You don't even have an invite to the De Leon," she said to him sternly, her British accent at full throttle. "It is by very special invitation only, you know."

"I'll get an invite," Tobey told her confidently. "Believe me, Monarch is going to want this car in the race."

"But no one knows where the race is going to be," Julia said. "At least until you get the invite. So exactly where would you be racing off to?"

Tobey looked back over at Benny, who smirked.

"Should I tell her?" Benny asked him.

"Be my guest," Tobey replied.

"On the down low," Benny said to Julia in a sort of conspiratorial whisper, "we've been doing some spying over the past couple months, and we know the De Leon will be in California this year. We just don't know where. But we know one of the drivers, and—"

"Benny!" Tobey half-yelled at him. "Loose lips . . ."

Benny got the hint. He shut up in mid-sentence.

Julia just shook her head at the two of them. She was trying not to laugh.

"I admire your sense of adventure," she said. "I have a little brother who is afflicted with the same thing."

"And your point is?" Tobey asked her.

"California's a big state," she replied. "And you might remember my affinity for numbers? I'm a math gal."

"And what's your math saying?" Tobey asked her.

She smiled again. "The drivers' meeting is always the night before the race," she said. "So you have less than forty-five hours to get from New York to somewhere in California . . ."

"That's right," Tobey said. "So?"

Again, all she could do was shake her head at him.

"Let me see if I've got this right," she said. "Not only will you be violating your parole by leaving the state of New York, you're planning on driving for two days straight?"

Tobey nodded simply. "And your problem with that is?"

"Just that we better get going," she replied, surprising him. "It's actually forty-five hours and counting."

Tobey held his hands up.

"Whoa," he said. "You're not going anywhere. That's not part of the plan."

She didn't back down for an instant.

"You need a right-seater," she told him. "And, more important, Ingram is not leaving this car in the hands of an ex-con."

But Tobey was having none of it.

"No way," he said, shaking his head. "It's out of the question. First of all, I don't need you, and second, it's on me to fix this car if I damage it."

"And it's on me to keep you honest," she shot right back at him. "Now, there's forty-four hours and fifty-nine minutes left. So, let's go."

With that, Julia got back into the car and slammed the door shut. Tobey was flustered. He looked at Benny pleadingly. But Benny didn't know what to do.

"Maybe we can shake her at a fuel stop?" Tobey half whispered to his friend.

"Okay, no worries, boss," Benny replied under his breath. "I'll help you dump her. But she's right—we're already behind. So let's deal with it on the fly. I mean, at least she seems smart."

Tobey was still shaking his head, though. "I know she's smart," he said. "And also fucking gorgeous. But I just don't think I can't take it. All the . . . the . . ." Tobey used his hand to imitate a puppet chattering on endlessly.

Benny imitated the hand-puppet idea, saying, "You want me to dump her, boss? Yes, please. Then follow me, I will take you on the ride from hell. She will be begging to get out of that car. Word to the moms. Word to the moms."

Benny smacked Tobey on the back and walked away. Tobey thought over the insult for a moment.

Then he climbed into the driver's side of the Mustang. He felt a ripple of electricity shoot through him. This car; this beautiful car. He never really thought he'd ever see it again, never mind be back behind the wheel. But here he was. Sometimes prayers are answered.

He looked at Julia—she was smiling broadly back at him. He couldn't help it—he smiled, too, briefly.

Then he started the Mustang's massive engine, revving it twice, and off they went.

**Part
Five**

Twelve

▊▊▊▊▊▊▊▊▊▊▊▊▊▊▊▊▊▊▊▊▊▊▊▊▊▊▊▊▊▊▊

THE SUPER MUSTANG crossed the George Washington Bridge less than twenty minutes later.

What was usually a forty-five-minute drive down from Mount Kisco to Manhattan had been done in half that time by the awesome Shelby GT.

Tobey was settled in behind the wheel, still buzzing with the twin excitements of driving this car again and being out of the clink. The Mustang had not lost any of its power or its balls. He was casually blowing by any slower traffic he encountered, which was actually all of it. Or, if anything posed any kind of impediment to him, he simply cut around it.

This was literally life in the fast lane. He'd averaged 120 mph since leaving Mount Kisco, and hit 130 as soon as they crossed the border into New Jersey.

He'd had little conversation with Julia so far, mostly because she'd been too busy holding on for dear life. But once they'd reached the New Jersey Turnpike, Tobey finally turned to her and said, "Okay, so you've never been a right-seater before."

She gave him a quick, icy glare.

"Don't worry," she replied over the roar of the Mustang's mighty engine. "I'll learn. And if you see something I'm doing wrong, please just point it out."

Tobey laughed. "Well, for one thing, you're wearing high heels," he said.

She just shook her head.

"We call them 'heels' these days," she said. "And I have a change of shoes in my overnight bag."

"Then I suggest you do something about that," Tobey said.

Julia reached into her overnight bag, retrieved some more sensible shoes, and changed them with the heels.

"There," she said. "Anything else 'right-seaters' are meant to do?"

Tobey replied tartly, "How about 'be quiet'?"

Julia continued glaring at him. "Like a mouse, you mean?"

"Yeah, like a dead mouse," Tobey said.

She began to say something, but stopped. He stared straight ahead, knowing that one might have cut a little too deep.

A chilly silence enveloped the car, and it stayed that way for a long time.

*   *   *

High above the New Jersey Turnpike, a Cessna Skyhawk was cruising at 130 mph, closely following the same direction of the highway as it headed south.

Benny was at the plane's controls.

He clicked his microphone on.

"Beauty," he said. "This is Maverick. I've just found you. And you've got a situation a mile ahead."

"Roger that," Tobey replied via the Mustang's two-way radio. "Copy a situation one mile ahead."

He pushed up to another gear and exploded down the highway. He was soon traveling at 140 mph.

"We've got bad traffic up ahead," he said to Julia, finally breaking the silence. "We've got to reroute."

She was mystified. "But I don't see any traffic," she said, sitting up in her seat and trying to see the road up ahead.

"We don't," Tobey said, pointing skyward. "But Benny does. He can see everything—he's our spy in the sky. And I've got to listen to him. Hold on . . ."

The two-way radio crackled again. "Stop and go traffic ahead," Benny reported. "I'm looking for an exit for you."

Julia was puzzled.

"You're going to hit traffic on this trip," she said matter-of-factly. "*Every* city has traffic. Won't that be a big problem?"

"Under the best conditions, we need to average just over 80 miles an hour to get to Cali in time," Tobey told her. "But for every hour we lose, we'll need to go 160 miles an hour to make it up. So yes, there will be traffic. It's just up to us to avoid it as much as possible."

Benny's voice came back on the radio.

"Give me a dollar on the next exit," he told Tobey.

"What's a dollar?" Julia asked.

Tobey smiled. "You'll see," he said.

He quickly upshifted, and a moment later, the Mustang was screaming down the breakdown lane, heading toward an off-ramp. At just the right moment, Tobey hit the brakes, drifted to the right, and took the exit going 100 mph—aka "a dollar."

Julia's education on the monetary term came with a price. With one hand holding tightly to the dash, the other tightly to the door, she turned a little green at the sudden, violent deceleration and then *acceleration*.

The Mustang rocketed up the off-ramp.

Benny's voice came back again. "Okay, go hard right for lane three in three . . . two . . . one . . ."

This sounded like Greek to Julia, too, but she was quickly realizing that Tobey and Benny were using a precise shorthand language to converse with each other.

Each lane of the highway was numbered one through four. All Benny had to do was say one of those numbers and Tobey would know immediately what lane would be freest of traffic or delay. What fascinated Julia the most, though, was how this language showed the tight bond between the two friends. Traveling in excess of 100 mph Tobey would switch lanes totally on blind faith.

It was crazy, but admirable, too.

At the end of the off-ramp, Tobey burned through the intersection and turned right onto a three-lane, one-way street.

Benny's voice crackled over the radio again: "We need to get you clean," he told Tobey. "Hard left U in three . . . two . . . one . . ."

Tobey steered the Mustang violently to the left, executing a perfect 180-degree turn. He suddenly rocketed into a car wash.

Benny kept talking. "Soft right through the full service bay and then go hard right."

The Mustang roared out of the car wash and turned right. Suddenly they were going straight into the oncoming traffic.

Benny yelled, "Go, three . . . now!"

With a flick of his wrist, Tobey zipped the Mustang into the slow lane of the oncoming traffic. They were heading toward a merging intersection. Those cars coming in the opposite direction that saw the Mustang speeding toward them immediately stopped or got out of the way. For his part, Tobey weaved around them with remarkable skill.

Julia was trying desperately to maintain a poker face throughout all this harrowing maneuvering. But it was hard to do. Everything was going by so fast.

Suddenly the rear of a stopped SUV was looming large in the Mustang's windshield.

"You do see the SUV you're about to plow into, right?" she asked Tobey as calmly as possible.

Instantly, Tobey jerked the Mustang into an oncoming lane, just missing the back of the SUV.

"You mean that SUV?" he asked her with a smirk. "The white one?"

That crisis passed—but another immediately took its place. A large commuter bus was heading right at them.

"Maintain speed," Benny calmly advised from above, even though that speed was 100 mph on a very crowded street.

The bus flashed its lights madly as the driver went into a sudden full-blown panic. The Mustang was heading right at it, now topping 105 mph.

"And the bus?" Julia asked Tobey urgently. "You see *that*, don't you?"

"What's that?" he replied.

"The *bus* . . ." she repeated urgently, her voice rising in tone.

"The *what*?" Tobey asked again.

Julia finally lost it.

"The bus!" she yelled. "The bus! *The bus!*"

She braced for impact—but Tobey maintained his cool. The front of the bus filled the windshield. The driver blew his horn again. Julia screamed loudly, almost drowning out everything else.

Then, from above, came Benny's voice: "Go, two, *now*!"

Tobey swerved right, missing a head-on collision with the oncoming bus by inches. And suddenly that crisis had passed as well.

Julia took a deep breath and tried hard to regain her composure. Tobey glanced over at her.

"You mean that bus, bus, bus?" he asked her.

But Julia refused to take the bait. She put her poker face back on and just stared straight ahead.

Then, from Benny again: "Hard left in three . . ."

Tobey downshifted, resulting in a violent deceleration. At the same moment, Julia's cell phone began ringing. But it was somewhere behind the front seat. She undid her seat belt, turned around, knelt on the seat, and began searching for it.

It was ringing urgently, yet she couldn't find it.

"Shit—where is it?" she cursed.

From Benny: ". . . two . . . one . . . now!"

The Mustang went across three lanes of traffic in less than three seconds, blowing through a red light for good measure.

"Give me a dollar for a quarter," Benny then requested from on high.

Leaving the traffic behind, the Mustang went back to accelerating. It was soon tearing down a one-lane rural road.

But Julia was still upset.

"You and Benny have this cheeky language," she said, still facing backward and kneeling on the seat. "You think it's adorable, do you? Well, it's not! If I'm going to help you, I need to know what you're saying!"

She launched into a near-perfect imitation of their strong, upstate New York, thoroughly American accents.

"Gimme a dollar!" she said. "Roger that! Soft right! Three, two, one! You need to speak *English*, Tobey."

But at that moment, still traveling at 110 mph, the Mustang hit a huge speed bump. The supercar went airborne, all four tires leaving the ground. Julia went airborne as well, ass over teakettle, landing in a heap on the front-seat floor.

Tobey couldn't resist. He called up to Benny and asked, "Are you having fun up there yet?"

"Roy Rogers," was Benny's reply. "Hard left in ten . . ."

Just as Julia was crawling back into her seat, Tobey downshifted and slid through the upcoming intersection. Amid a gaggle of traffic, he also managed to turn a hard left.

Benny radioed down: "On-ramp in three . . . two . . . one . . ."

Tobey hit the ramp, topping 112 mph.

The radio crackled again. "Okay, Beauty," Benny said finally. "You're all clear from here."

Julia's eyes were firing daggers at Tobey by this point. But he stayed quiet, as if nothing unusual had happened.

"I understand that driving fast is going to be necessary," she half-yelled at him. "But driving like some mental patient just to scare me out of the car is not going to work."

"Are you sure about that?" Tobey asked her.

"Well, if that's what you thought," she said to him angrily, "then, whatever you think of me, I'm sure it's wrong."

Tobey just stared straight ahead. "Then educate me," he finally told her.

And so she did.

"So you think," she began, "that just because I make a living buying cars designed to triple the speed limit, and drive a Maserati—and oh, by the way, I am an awesome driver—that you can condescend to me? If you think that, then I guarantee you, this will be the longest forty-four hours and eleven minutes of your life."

Tobey almost laughed at her. He'd spent many months in solitary confinement. He knew well what a "long" forty-four hours could feel like.

But then he thought about it a moment, and finally said, "One request? You talk less."

"I know," she replied. "Like a dead mouse?"

She put on a high, mouse-like voice and continued, "*Squeak, squeak—here I am. I'm a mouse—I'm dying. I'm dead. I'm a dead mouse and I'm not talking now.* Right? Like that?"

Tobey couldn't help it. He smiled a bit.

She is very *cute,* he thought.

Now that the atmosphere inside the Mustang was eased a bit, Tobey laid on the gas and headed for the western horizon, still traveling in excess of a dollar.

Thirteen

THE RESTAURANT WAS one of the most expensive in the country.

In one corner, at the best table in the place, were Dino, Anita, and a man and wife. The man was a multimillionaire and, even better for Dino, he was an investor. This meant he was a mark for Dino. A person from whom he could siphon money. A sucker.

That was the underlying reason for the dinner. Doing her part as Dino's arm candy was Anita, who looked stunning.

"Believe me," the investor was telling Dino, "I'm not trying to be an asshole."

"You don't have to try that hard," his wife interjected in a perfect deadpan, sipping her drink.

"It's just that the idea of a guy called 'Monarch,'" the

investor went on, a bit uncertain, "and that he hosts a secret race and all? Well, it's just a bit hard to believe."

Dino nodded sympathetically. "He's supposedly from a blue-blood, wealthy family," he said. "Real old money. People who made their fortunes during the industrial revolution."

"And no one knows who he is?" the investor asked.

Dino shook his head. "No one," he said.

"Well, Dino does," Anita said, suddenly interrupting.

Dino looked at her. He was both surprised and amused.

"Oh, I do?" he asked.

"It's just a feeling I get," she said.

"You calling me a liar?" Dino asked her.

"Sometimes I think you're not telling the whole story," she replied.

Dino waved her quiet, then turned back to his dinner companions.

"Monarch has sponsored Formula 1 race teams," Dino told them. "Always under other names. But *that* I know about him for sure."

"Really an underground type," the man's wife said.

"With a bad ticker," Dino said. "Word is, he used to drive in big races, but he could drop dead at any moment, so he quit the hands-on racing business."

Dino knew the mark was warming up, though it might have been the alcohol.

"I'd love to see his podcast," he said.

"Monarch's site is private," Anita told him. "It's by invite only."

Dino took a long swig of his scotch. *Wonder when she'll shut up,* he thought.

"What's the prize for the De Leon?" the mark asked.

"Big rewards come with big risks," Dino answered. "Any car that's in the race and loses automatically belongs to the winner. I won it last year and left with more than six million dollars in cars. And one of them was a new Pagani."

"Sounds like a good day's work," the man said with a laugh.

"Yes, it was," Dino replied, turning mock serious. "But listen, I'm not trying to push you—however, I've got another interested party. Now, I'm not a hundred percent sure about them. You know that feeling?"

"I know it well," the mark replied. "And I liked what I saw at your garage. That's quite a dealership you've got going there. The problem I have is you haven't shown a hard profit yet, at least not in cash."

Dino shifted uncomfortably in his chair. Frustration was starting to show around the edges of his face.

"Let me be blunt," he said. "What do I have to do to get a real commitment from you?"

"I'll be blunt right back," the investor replied. "What do you consider a 'real commitment'?"

"Five million," Dino said. "With that kind of money, we can be one of the biggest high-end car dealerships in the country."

"Win this 'secret' De Leon again, then," the investor said.

"You mean, if I win this year's De Leon," Dino said, "you're in for five million?"

The man reached over the table and shook Dino's hand. "Yes, I am," he said.

"Can I get that in writing?" Dino asked him.

"Just send me a contract," the man replied.

The couple was gone a few minutes later. Once they were out of sight, Dino collapsed back into his chair. He sucked down what was left of his scotch and then tossed the glass back on the table.

"I *need* that guy," he said worriedly. "I *need* that deal."

Anita was surprised to hear this.

"What do you mean?" she asked him. "You told me your dealership made a big profit last year."

"It's paper profit," Dino told her dismissively. "I need some fresh cash to survive."

He looked away from her, his features turning dark. Anita continued staring at him, though.

At that point, she really didn't know what to think.

Fourteen

NIGHT HAD FALLEN on Ohio.

The Shelby Mustang roared down the highway, relentlessly heading west, traveling more than twice the speed of those few cars and trucks sharing the dark road with it.

Tobey was driving in silence—at 120 mph. Julia was asleep. It was almost midnight. He punched a number into his iPhone.

Joe Peck's voice came on immediately. "Checking in," he said.

"Mile marker four seventeen," Tobey replied. "We're on schedule."

Joe Peck was driving alone in a vehicle they all called the Beast. It was the team's support truck. Big and boxy, it looked like a combination tow truck and delivery van. It was full of spare tires, parts, water, batteries, oil, and transmission fluid—everything they might need during the high-speed cross-country dash. But it also carried the most important thing of all: fuel.

"It's a miracle that we're still on schedule," Joe told Tobey. "Maybe we have an outside chance of actually pulling this thing off. I was just sitting here thinking, 'Pete would have loved this trip.'"

The words hit Tobey right in the gut. "Yeah," he replied sadly. "He loved the impossible."

"Dino should be in jail for what he did to Pete that day," Joe said.

"I'll never forget what I saw when I found him," Tobey replied. "I still have nightmares about it . . ."

"*He* wrecked him, Tobey," Joe went on. "*He* picked him and flipped him. Let me ask you . . . what if you get behind Dino's back bumper? What if you end up back there in the race? What will *you* do?"

Tobey thought deeply about what Joe was asking him—and not for the first time. But he didn't reply. His silence said it all.

"That's what I thought," Joe said. "Okay, brother, I'll see you in Detroit. Beast out."

Still mulling over his conversation with Joe, Tobey glanced at Julia. He expected to find her still sleeping.

But he got a surprise. She was wide awake and looking right at him.

"I'm sorry about Pete," she told him. "I only met him those two times. Remember? At the exhibit hall in Manhattan and then the next day at the Shepperton Racetrack.

But I could tell what kind of person he was just by his smile. He reminded me of my own little brother. Always in motion. Always smiling—a real pest, he is. But I love him to death."

"Dino just left him there," Tobey said angrily. "That's what I can't forgive. The trial, the prison, everything that happened. None of that would even matter to me if Pete were still alive. I realize what we do isn't pretty, but there is one unwritten rule: You *always* go back."

"That's what this is really all about?" Julia asked him. "To somehow avenge Pete's death?"

Tobey didn't reply. He didn't want to. He just fixed his gaze back on the road and kept on driving.

Fifteen

IT WAS FRIDAY, nearly 8:00 a.m., and heavy morning traffic was clogging the streets of downtown Detroit, as usual.

Inside one of the many buildings in the downtown area, one office was particularly busy. Phones were ringing, mail was being delivered to people working in endless rows of cubicles. This fourth-floor office was full of hustle and bustle.

Finn was sitting in one of these cubicles, feeling not unlike a rat in a maze. He was dressed in business attire, a far cry from his grease-monkey days back at Marshall Motors.

His iPhone suddenly rang. He looked at the caller's number, shook his head, and let it go to voice mail. But then the iPhone rang again. This time, he picked it up.

It was Joe Peck.

"We've already had this conversation," Finn told him plainly.

"Just go to the window," Joe replied.

"No," Finn said. "Why would I do that?"

"Just go, now," Joe insisted.

Finn just shook his head again. Then he got up and walked to the window.

He looked down to the street below and was surprised to see the Shelby Mustang idling loudly on the curb right outside his office building. Even in a place called Motor City, the car stood out, a stark contrast to the fuel-efficient, home-by-five cars making up most of the morning rush hour around it.

The Mustang's engine started to rev higher. It was incredibly loud—so much so, it could be heard four stories up. Half the people in Finn's office immediately rushed to the windows to see what was making the racket.

Down inside the supercar, Julia was mystified, as always.

"What are you doing?" she asked Tobey as he continued revving the engine with earsplitting results.

"Just keeping the engine hot," he replied.

She looked around them—the crowded streets, the crowded sidewalks. Everyone was looking at them.

"Do you really want to be attracting so much attention?" she asked him. "You are on the run from the law, you know."

Tobey didn't reply. He just smiled mischievously.

A moment later a Detroit police cruiser pulled up next to the Mustang.

The officer inside rolled down his window and yelled over to Tobey.

"This your car, son?" the officer asked.

"Are you crazy?" Tobey yelled back to him. "This is a one-of-a-kind car. Do you know how expensive it is?"

The cop straightened up in his seat. He didn't need this so early in the morning. He immediately tagged Tobey as being a problem.

"Why don't you pull it around the corner," he told Tobey. "We can have a talk."

But Tobey ignored his request.

Instead he yelled back. "Did you see how fast I was going?" he asked the cop. "It was like 160 miles per hour on that off-ramp back there. Insane! You gotta drive this car."

While all this was happening, Tobey was secretly taping himself and Julia on his iPad.

"I'm sorry, officer," Julia yelled over to the cop. "I think my boyfriend is just showing off to impress me."

The cop was growing increasingly exasperated. "Just pull it around the corner," he yelled back.

Tobey rolled up the window.

" 'Boyfriend'?" he said to Julia.

"I'm just trying to keep us out of jail," she replied seriously.

"If it's getting too hot for you," he told her, "you should probably get out now."

"Are you kidding?" she exclaimed. "This is my car!"

"It's *Ingram's* car," Tobey corrected her. "And, by the way, you may want to fix your hair."

"For my mug shot, you mean?" she asked.

Tobey tapped the iPad, switching the POV to film what was happening through the windshield.

"No," he finally replied. "But I *am* about to make you famous."

Finn was watching all this from his fourth-floor office window, wondering what the hell was going on. It was almost magical to see the Shelby Mustang again. And he had no doubt who was behind the wheel—but what was Tobey up to? Joe was still on the phone with him.

"That's not exactly the part I wanted you to see," Joe told him. "But just watch how the car leans when it pulls away from the cop."

Not a moment later the Mustang screamed away from the curb. It took off with so much force, it was going sideways. There was a storm of smoke and dust—and lots of earsplitting DBs.

The lights on top of the police car came to life. With siren wailing, it was instantly off in pursuit of the Mustang.

And suddenly, Finn was enjoying the little drama four stories below.

"Wow, that Mustang is loose, man," he said to Joe Peck. He was seeing what the Shelby could do for the first time.

"I know," Joe replied. "And if Tobey runs that setup at De Leon, well—"

"He's in the race, you mean?" Finn interrupted.

"He's about to be," Joe replied, a little mysteriously.

"What the hell does that mean?" Finn wanted to know.

"It means he's about to be," Joe said again.

Finn's phone clicked. "Gotta go," he told Joe. "Tobey's calling."

Finn clicked over to answer Tobey's call. While Tobey was, at that moment, driving the Mustang around in a loud, noisy circle, cop car behind him, siren screaming, trying to chase him, he was still somehow able to talk.

"I need you, buddy," Tobey yelled to Finn over all the commotion.

But Finn stayed silent as he watched the cop car chase the Mustang round and round.

Tobey continued. "Finn . . . brother?" he said. "I know you're there . . . Okay, I'll do the talking. I get why you left. It got nuts. It got nuts for all of us. But right now we're doing something really stupid, and we really need you. It's not Marshall Motors without you."

Finn took a deep breath and thought long and hard about what Tobey was telling him.

Finally, he hung up the phone and said to himself, "This is a big mistake . . ."

Then he walked to the elevator, pushed the down button—and began taking off his clothes.

People in the cubicles nearby stood to watch him. First Finn removed his shirt and folded it neatly, revealing his bony, bare chest. More people in his office took notice. Then he took off his pants and folded them along with the shirt. Then came the boxers—and just like that, except for his socks, Finn was naked.

He waited calmly for the elevator. It arrived with a loud *ding!*

That's when he turned back to his coworkers and said, "Have a nice day."

The door elevator opened to reveal the car was crowded. Somehow, Finn managed to squeeze in.

The passengers were horrified, but no one said a word. Finn found himself standing next to an older, smaller woman.

"My friend is running the fastest Mustang in the world at the De Leon race on Sunday," he told her.

The woman smiled at him and said, "I'm in accounting."

"But don't you feel like you're dying inside?" Finn asked her.

She didn't stop smiling. "Yes," she replied. "Yes, I do."

She glanced down at his nether regions and frowned. A frightened turtle came to mind.

Finn was immediately defensive.

"Hey, it's cold in here," he said.

A moment later, the elevator door opened into the lobby. Joe Peck was waiting there. He saw Finn walk out of the elevator, nude except for his socks.

Joe couldn't believe it. "No freaking way!" he exclaimed.

"Where's the Beast?" Finn asked him nonchalantly.

"On the street," Joe replied. "C'mon, we gotta roll."

Joe hustled Finn through the lobby. Many eyes were falling on them—though mostly on Finn. One woman took out her phone and made a hasty call. A guy in a suit applauded and started snapping pictures.

"Why did you nude it up?" Joe asked his friend.

Finn just shrugged. "I figured if I got balls-out naked in front of all my coworkers, I'd be too embarrassed to ever go back."

"So, you just left your clothes up there?" Joe asked him.

"Yeah," Finn replied. "Along with my dignity."

Meanwhile, Tobey was driving very hard and fast and no longer going around in circles.

He was screaming through the crowded streets of Detroit, making a lot of noise and getting a lot of attention. Luckily he was at his best in these kinds of situations. Checking mirrors. Effortlessly shifting up and down. Laying on the gas, using the brakes only when absolutely necessary.

A second police car had joined the chase. But this only added to the excitement. Then came some positive news from Joe Peck.

"I've got the package," Tobey heard Joe say over the iPhone. "And we're out the back door."

"That's great news!" Tobey replied. "But we've only got twenty-eight hours to get to Cali."

That's when Julia spotted something above them. It was a helicopter with "WLTV Channel 4" emblazoned on its side. It went right over the top of the speeding Mustang.

"I'm afraid we've got company," she said.

Tobey's phone rang an instant later. He answered it to hear an unexpected, but familiar, voice.

"WLTV Channel 4 News with a question for Tobey Marshall," the voice crackled. "On a scale of one to ten, how crazy hot is your passenger?"

Tobey and Julia looked over at the helicopter, which was now flying almost level with the Mustang.

To their surprise, they saw Benny saluting them from the cockpit.

"Like my new ride?" Benny asked. "Bitchin', right?"

Tobey couldn't believe it—and neither could Julia.

"What happened to the Cessna?" Tobey asked him.

"They have flight restrictions over the city, bro," Benny replied. "So I had to borrow my buddy's little whirly bird."

Tobey expertly drifted the Mustang into a right-hand turn and zoomed into an alleyway. The cops were still right on his tail, lights flashing, sirens blaring, but they knew they had their hands full with a driver like him.

So their plan was to trap him. One cop car followed him into the alley, while the other entered from the opposite end. Tobey immediately slammed on the brakes and began backing up.

"Oh boy," Tobey said, flooring the Mustang in reverse. "This might get interesting."

Meanwhile, Finn was inside the Beast pulling on some of Joe's extra clothes. Suddenly Benny's voice came blasting through the supply truck's two-way radio.

"Listen up, guys," Benny began. "I almost borrowed an Apache chopper from the Great Lakes Air Base—but Colonel Gatins was sweating me hard."

Joe Peck just rolled his eyes.

"Here we go again," he said.

Finn yelled into the microphone. "Enough with the Apache helicopter bullshit. Give it a fucking rest!"

"I'm not talking to you, Finn-ski," Benny yelled back.

"Roger that, Liar One," Finn retorted.

Benny's voice went up a notch.

"Finn, you've been back in the crew for ten minutes and you're already up my skirt, talking shit," the pilot scolded him. "You're going to rue the day you started calling me that."

Finn laughed. " 'Rue the day'?" he asked. "What, did you go to college all of a sudden?"

"That's an ignorant thing to say," Benny shot back. "God, are you ignorant!"

Tobey and Julia were listening to the chatter between the crewmates, all while the Mustang was furiously going down the alley—in reverse.

Julia couldn't believe what she was hearing.

"Are you kidding me?" she said to Tobey. "Are these guys still in elementary school?"

Tobey smiled as he finally backed out of the alley at 70 mph and headed up another street—in the wrong direction, of course.

"Is it going to be like this the whole way?" Julia asked him.

Tobey just shrugged as he upshifted and laid on the accelerator.

"We've all known each other for a very long time," he told her.

"That's a 'yes,' then," she huffed.

Benny's voice interrupted them.

"Beauty—this is Maverick," he began. "The Motown Mounties really want to speak with you. Come back."

Tobey was maneuvering fiercely now, swerving around the oncoming traffic, while noticing that a third police cruiser had joined the chase. Just as he was about to hit one civilian car head-on, he downshifted and hit the brakes and the gas, all at the same time. The result was a perfect reverse 270-degree turn.

When the smoke cleared, he found himself facing the right way down Michigan Avenue. He laid down the hammer again, taking off like a rocket. This caused the first cruiser to collide with the second one, putting both out of action. The third one, though, kept up the pursuit.

Tobey did another hard drift and wound up in the city's waterfront district.

He was now topping 100 mph, but the third police car was gaining on him.

Up in the news copter, Benny heard another voice come on his radio. It was distinctly female.

"Romeo, stand by," it said.

"Standing by," Benny said, with some uncertainty.

He had moved the copter's traffic cam off the roadways and onto a hot-looking female running along the waterfront park. Just for kicks, he zoomed in.

As it turned out, the strange voice was coming from the Channel 4 newsroom.

He heard it again. It said: "We go live to Romeo in the Channel 4 traffic chopper. How are we looking, Romeo?"

Benny replied in a typical TV announcer voice.

"We're looking good, Beth," he said. "Real good."

But then a producer's voice interrupted, "Is that Romeo in that helicopter? What's going on?"

At that moment, the copter cam pulled into an extremely tight shot of the jogger's derriere.

Immediately, the producer started screaming, "Commercial! Go to a commercial!"

Benny just laughed.

"Hey, Motown, gotta lighten up," he said.

As all this was going on, Tobey found himself hurtling toward a huge bridge.

"Eyes on the road," he told himself aloud.

Benny saw the long span at the same time.

"Whoa, I think that's the Ambassador Bridge," he yelled. "And it's filled with the bumper-to-bumper."

He pulled back on the copter's controls, putting the machine into a near-hover.

"Tobey, brother," he called down to the Mustang. "It's going to take a three-lane grasshopper to disappear. Do you copy?"

Tobey was quick to reply: "I copy."

"Okay," Benny said. "On my count, then . . . three . . . two . . . one . . ."

The Mustang hit the I-375 on-ramp at tremendous speed. This despite lots of traffic everywhere—and a cop car, siren wailing, right behind it.

Julia took her usual crash position, and braced for impact.

"What's a grasshopper?" she yelled over at Tobey.

Tobey did not have time to answer. He jerked the speeding car into the on-ramp's fast lane. Up ahead, but getting closer very quickly, there was a huge embankment just before the entrance to the bridge itself.

"You might want to close your eyes," Tobey warned her.

Julia held on tighter, if that was possible.

"Oh my god," she screamed. "Is it worse than 'bus bus bus'?"

Benny's voice came over the radio. "Aim for that light pole," he told Tobey. "Then spread your wings . . ."

At those words, Tobey jerked the car out of the fast lane and up the embankment toward the light pole. He put the gas pedal to the floor . . . and suddenly, they were airborne.

Julia's eyes nearly fell out of her head. They were flying over three lanes of traffic, the Mustang's tires nearly clipping the roofs of the cars below. But before she had a chance to scream again or say anything else, they were suddenly back down, landing with a resounding *thump!* on the slope of a church parking lot. Without missing a beat, Tobey drifted violently across the grass, across the lot, and onto another street.

He straightened out the Mustang and downshifted for more RPMs.

Then he turned to look at Julia, expecting her to be in a state of shock or worse. But she was completely opposite of how Tobey thought she'd be.

She wasn't hurt or stunned or nauseous. Instead, she was laughing hysterically.

"We're *alive*!" she screamed with pure joy. "Amazing! You are *amazing*!"

Tobey almost started laughing himself—her laugh was sweet and funny and nearly contagious.

"It's what I do," he said in a perfect deadpan.

The Mustang roared down the street at an extremely high speed, heading away from Motor City.

High above, Benny had been looking down on the display of incredible extreme driving and admiring Tobey's out-of-this-world talent.

But now he had to go.

"Time's up in this bird," he radioed down to Tobey. "Talk soon, bro."

But Detroit wasn't giving up so easily.

One of the pursuing cops was especially pissed off. His patrol car had been involved in the accident that Tobey's wild driving had caused, and that made him mad.

He was now burning up his radio.

"All units be advised," the cop said. "Heavily modified silver Ford Mustang last seen on I-375 heading westbound. Contact state police for air support."

Sixteen

DETROIT REGIONAL AIRPORT was a very busy place this morning.

Many commuter planes were taking off and landing—some small airliners, too. The airport's helicopter section was especially humming. Private helicopters as well as TV news choppers were coming and going with great frequency. Support personnel and ground crews were dashing about, servicing the flock of whirlybirds.

It was in the middle of this hubbub that Benny managed to land the Channel 4 news copter. He came down hard, the chopper's rotors crying loudly until he mercifully cut the engines. Then he jumped out of the copter and sprinted away unscathed.

It took him only a minute to get back to his Cessna, which was parked nearby. He climbed in, did his prep-sheet, and then went to turn the engine over. But it misfired—two loud bangs, and then nothing.

He tried again, with the same result.

"Goddamn," he cursed, not wanting to attract any more attention to himself. "Why are you being cranky now?"

Meanwhile, out of his sight behind him, a state police helicopter was taking off.

It quickly went up to two thousand feet, beginning its routine traffic patrol. But suddenly its radio came to life.

"All air units be advised," the dispatcher said. "Be on the lookout for a silver Mustang with New York plates: Alpha, Delta, Tango, four, six, one, niner, heading west on I-94. Repeat, silver Mustang, heading west on I-94 . . ."

The pilots acknowledged the call and then turned south, pointing the copter's nose toward the interstate.

At the same moment, Tobey was roaring down Route I-94, free of pursuing authorities. But he was getting an uneasy feeling.

He hit upload on his iPad and tried to call Benny.

"Liar One? I've got the feeling we're going to have an air bear sniffing our tail soon," he said. "Are you tracking anything like that heading toward I-94? If he spots me then the game is over."

But there was no immediate reply from Benny. Tobey radioed the same message again. Finally Benny's voice came on.

"I'm still on the ground, Beauty," he reported to Tobey. "This Motown air is making my bird a little cranky."

Tobey could hear him urging the Cessna to turn over.

"Come on, Nelly," Benny was saying. "We got things to do."

But the engine just wouldn't cooperate, and Benny told him so.

This was not good and Tobey knew it. He called the Beast. Finn came on the line. He and Joe were also heading west on I-94.

"Benny is grounded for the moment," Tobey told them. "And that means we're blind to the air bears. We might have to go to Plan B."

"Roger, Beauty," Finn answered. "But be advised, Plan B adds at least an hour to the trip."

"We've got no choice," Tobey told him. "We'll just have to make up the time later."

"Roger that," Finn said soberly.

"Beauty will have to go bingo first," Tobey said. "We need to hot fuel and top off."

"Understand, Beauty," Finn replied. "Hot fuel and top off. See you at the bingo point."

Once again, Julia was looking at Tobey with her quizzical face.

"What?" he asked her.

"'Hot fuel'?" she asked back. "'Top off'? 'Bingo'?"

"We're refueling without stopping," he told her simply.

"Really?" she replied. "That sounds rather . . . well, 'inspired.' But can't you just say that?"

Tobey actually considered her suggestion.

She certainly likes the basics, he thought.

The Beast was flying down Route I-94, now about fifty miles west of Detroit.

Joe Peck was still at the wheel of the ungainly truck; Finn was in the passenger's seat. Somewhere on the highway behind it, but getting closer all the time, was the Shelby Mustang.

Joe Peck checked their position via the truck's GPS module and then said to Finn, "Get ready—it's showtime."

Finn immediately unbuckled his seat belt. Then he took a deep breath, opened his door, and began climbing out of the truck—all as it was roaring down the highway at 70 mph.

"Hot fuel coming up," Joe Peck said into his iPhone.

He looked in his rearview mirror to see the silver Mustang suddenly appear right in back of him.

"On time," Joe said. "And on the money."

Using great care and balance, Finn had climbed completely out of the door of the speeding truck and was now moving himself along its side panels. It took great effort, but he finally climbed over the panels and fell into the truck's rear bed.

Scrambling to the back corner, he dropped the tailgate to give himself more room to maneuver. There was a large gas tank back here with an extra long hose attached. The hose's nozzle was a special design. It looked like the long needle nose of a mosquito.

The Mustang moved up closer to the Beast, its powerful engine drowning out the noise being made by the rest of the traffic on the heavily traveled interstate.

Tobey carefully maneuvered the Shelby so the supercar's gas intake was right next to the Beast's tailgate. Holding this parallel formation, the two vehicles roared along the highway, still going 70 mph.

Military planes frequently took on fuel in flight, eliminating the need for them to land anytime they were low on gas. It took a lot of practice and training for the military pilots involved to get it right. The Marshall Motors crew was about to attempt the same thing, but while speeding along a highway. It was just as dangerous, though.

Tobey brought the Mustang closer to the Beast; he was just inches away now. But even though Finn was leaning way out over the roadway, needle-nose hose in hand, he could not reach the Mustang's gas tank cover.

Tobey had no choice. He brought the Mustang in even closer to the supply and Finn tried again—but still, it was no good. Finn just couldn't get close enough to flip the gas cover open.

Julia was watching all this with a mixture of horror and fascination. She knew how dangerous it was, as well as all the attention they were attracting. She also knew there was a state police helicopter up there somewhere, and it wouldn't take much for its pilots to spot these shenanigans from two thousand feet.

She knew she had to do something.

Suddenly she unbuckled her seat belt.

"What are you doing?" Tobey yelled over to her.

"Helping," she yelled back. "Or trying to."

Without another word, she put one leg out the open window and straddled the door for a moment. Then she climbed out. The wind immediately caught her hair and clothes and started whipping them furiously. Tobey was very shocked. He had no idea she had a stunt like this in her.

All the way out of the car now, Julia stretched as far as she could, and was just able to reach the Mustang's gas tank cover. With admirable dexterity, she flipped it open.

Throughout all this, Finn was looking at her like she was nuts. He reached out to hold her steady and prevent her from falling. With Finn's support, she was able to twist the gas cap off.

Finn immediately fit the needle nose into the fuel tank opening. Once it was connected, he hit the pump lever and the fuel started to flow from the Beast's holding tank into the Mustang.

Julia meanwhile reversed her direction and climbed back inside the Mustang. She was soon buckled back into her seat.

Tobey was in total disbelief.

"Wow," he said to her. "The hits just keep coming with you, don't they?"

Julia just shrugged good-naturedly.

"Don't judge a girl by her Guccis," she joked.

"Her what?" Tobey asked innocently.

She held up one of her expensive shoes.

" 'High heels'," she said, teasing him, then tossing the shoes behind the front seat. "Remember?"

"Can't you just say that?" Tobey teased her back.

"Nice one," she replied, with a slight bow of her head. "Touché."

Tobey quickly got back to business.

"Beast, take the shoulder," he radioed to Joe Peck. "I'll go with you."

"Roger that," Joe Peck replied.

The Beast, with the Mustang still attached by the fuel hose, moved onto the shoulder of the highway's slow lane. They passed an RV like it was standing still and then spotted a sign that read, "Parker Road South, Next Exit."

Julia was now watching the ongoing refueling operation out the window; she knew timing was an important element here. She gave Finn the "faster" sign, but he replied by holding up his hand, indicating her to wait.

Finn was closely watching the gas pump's gauge. He waited a few more seconds—it was crucial that the Mustang got every last drop of fuel he could give it. Then he finally flipped the lever to off. He yanked the needle-nose hose out of the fill spout and gave Julia the thumbs-up.

She returned the gesture, then yelled over to Tobey, "We're clear."

That's all Tobey needed to hear. He upshifted, then punched the gas pedal, and the Mustang rocketed ahead as if it had afterburners.

"You see," he said to Julia. "That was easy."

"Yes, indeed," she replied in her best Cockney accent. "And so is brain surgery."

It was here that the two vehicles split up. The Beast continued driving west on I-94. Tobey roared off the highway at the Parker Road South exit and down a secondary road.

Tobey called the Beast. "Thanks, boys—Plan B is a go-ahead. Beauty is now a redneck."

"Roger," Joe Peck replied. "Beast loves a redneck."

Julia figured this out quickly.

"Redneck," she said. "We're heading south?"

"Impressive," Tobey replied.

She smiled. "It's not a very tricky code, Tobey," she told him. "Truth be told."

Back in the Beast, Finn had returned to the truck's cab, reversing the same way he had gone out. He was wearing a huge smile.

"That was more fun than I've had in a long time," he told Joe.

Joe took this as his cue to put the hammer down, upshift, and accelerate. Their on-the-fly refueling mission was done.

"Welcome back," he told Finn.

A moment later, they both heard a roaring sound. Before either could react, the Michigan State Police helicopter went over the top of the Beast.

Finn was quickly on the radio.

"Liar One," he called. "Are you airborne yet? Come in!"

Finally Benny's voice came through the speaker.

"Just got up after spanking my engine for a while," he reported. "I'm heading in your direction at top speed."

"Well, you can slow down, because you just missed all the drama," Finn said. "We did the bingo right under the air bear's nose."

Benny laughed. "I'm sorry I missed it," he said. "But you have to admit, it was more fun that way, right?"

"Maybe from where you're sitting," Finn told him. "Beauty is on Plan B, but we'd still like eyes on that air bear."

Benny scanned the horizon and soon picked up a set of lights about two miles away. It was the state police helicopter, but it was turning. As Benny watched, the copter did a long loop and headed east, back in the direction of Detroit.

"I see your air bear," Benny reported. "And he's heading home to mama."

"Liar One, roger—that's good news, Liar One," Finn said, cracking up Joe in the process. "By the way, Liar One—what's your twenty?"

"Flat-hatting you, you bitch," Benny replied quickly.

In the next instant, the Cessna came out of nowhere and brutally buzzed the Beast, clearing it by just a few feet. Finn and Joe Peck ducked almost to the floorboards, it had happened so quick and so unexpectedly. They saw the bottom of the Cessna fill their windshield before it flew off again. It had been *very* close.

Finn barked at Benny, "Jesus Christ, are you insane? You haven't changed a bit, you fucking nimrod!"

Benny came back at him immediately. "I don't know who Nimrod is," he said. "But just keep this in mind unless you want to piss your drawers again: My *handle* is Maverick!"

Seventeen

FINALLY OFF THE hustle and bustle of the interstate, the Mustang was rocketing down a two-lane back road, passing vast stretches of farmland filled with crops, watering holes, and farm equipment.

Julia was beginning to get a handle on how to be a "right-seater." She'd started following police communications with a laser jammer dialed in. Using this device, which was built into the dashboard of the Mustang, it was possible to jam signals emitting from a radar gun. In other words, under the right conditions, the Mustang could become as invisible as a stealth fighter.

But she broke her focus on the high-tech anti-detection equipment when she felt Tobey staring at her.

She locked eyes with him and realized something

surprising just by the way he was looking at her. Tobey was smitten with her. She could see it all over his face.

"What?" she asked him coyly. "Were you going to say something to me?"

"Huh? No," Tobey replied awkwardly. "Nothing important."

"C'mon," she coaxed him. "It's okay."

He thought a moment and then asked, "I guess I was wondering, you know, how did you get involved in all this? The cars? The glamour?"

She laughed. "The glamour?"

She spread out her hands to indicate the rural setting they were driving through.

"I'm not sure the word 'glamour' applies at the moment," she added. "But if you want to know how I got here from there, well, I'll tell you—but try not to fall asleep at the wheel."

"I promise," he said.

"Okay," she said, with a sigh. "I grew up in England, obviously. My parents were hippies. Damn, my bloody grandparents were hippies! They were all very artistic and crunchy and organic—or at least they thought there were. There was always sixties music playing in our house when I was a kid. I was named after John Lennon's mother, you know. I was raised on granola and yogurt, and we only drank rainwater or melted snow. To this day I can't stomach yogurt, and I think granola is revolting. It's like chewing gravel, isn't it?"

"I hear you," Tobey replied.

She went on, "As you can imagine, I rebelled against all that as soon as I was old enough to realize that I could. I insisted that I go to a strict girls' boarding school. My goal was to learn all about business and mathematics and numbers and then go to work for the biggest mega-corporation on the planet. All this, just to toss off my parents.

"But then a strange thing happened. I started doodling in class one day—growing bored, you see—and that progressed to doing drawings and then I realized that I had some artistic talent in me, too. I had inherited it, quite to my surprise. But for some reason, I began drawing cars. Race cars. Bentleys. Lambos. I could see the artistic quality in their designs. By the time I left boarding school I was hooked.

"I went to university, took half business courses and half art classes, and when I got out, I went into the world of expensive cars, evaluating them, putting a price tag on them, not just for their performance but also for their beauty. I did it because it's what I loved, which is exactly why my parents and their parents did what they did. I had to grow up a bit to understand all that. Then, I met Ingram and . . ."

She looked out the window of the speeding Mustang, studying the American landscape going by in a blur.

"But just how I got here, to this point?" she asked herself. "I'm not quite sure yet."

Suddenly, the police radio began squawking. The police report was disturbing, though.

"All units be advised," the dispatcher said, "Ford Mustang, New York plate Alpha, Delta, Tango, four, six, one, niner, last seen headed west on I-94. Believed to be driven by one Tobey Marshall. Mike Alpha, Romeo, Sierra, Hotel, Alpha, Lima, Lima. Wanted on parole violation and possible grand theft auto. Spotted traveling with a blonde female, identity unknown."

"See what I mean?" she said. " 'Blonde female, identity unknown.' I'm just one step away from being a wanted woman."

Tobey shook his head in disgust. "Well, they know who I am now," he said. "But I guess that was just a matter of time."

"If it was, you sped it up with your little stunt back in Detroit," Julia told him.

"That had to be done," Tobey replied.

"Just to get Finn back in the fold?" she asked.

"No, not just that," he answered.

They were approaching an intersection, traveling at 100 mph. Suddenly, Tobey ripped a hard right, and an instant later they were traveling on Highway 12 West.

That's when the Monarch chirp sounded inside the Mustang. This meant the *Underground Racing* show's private streaming website was coming on live.

Monarch's voice crackled out of the speaker.

"I am looking at footage of a car that's not supposed to exist," he began in his usual droll way. "The trolls are lighting up my inbox, people telling me that this is the car that Ford and Shelby were building when Carroll died. Just like him, it's a ghost."

While he was saying this, Monarch began showing video of Tobey's stunt in Detroit in front of Finn's office building. The footage had been taken by Tobey's POV camera, and included aerial shots from Benny's helicopter escapade as well. Tobey and Benny had uploaded the footage practically as it was happening, and it eventually found its way to the *Underground Racing* show.

Monarch went on, "No one's ever really seen this car. No one with a bank account under one hundred million, that is. But it's gorgeous. Ford Motor Company birthed this baby and I'll be damned if it's not the finest Mustang I've ever seen. But here's the real news flash: Tobey Marshall is driving this chariot of the gods. Yes, the same Tobey Marshall who was tearing it up around Mount Kisco two years ago. I bow to Ford and Shelby for conceiving such a car. And I salute Tobey Marshall for what he's doing behind the wheel."

As Monarch spoke, he continued showing footage of Tobey's antics in Detroit, including him rocketing away from Finn's office with the Motor City police in hot pursuit.

Julia smiled and nodded in Tobey's direction. She understood now, and she had to give him his props—obviously he'd thought through every detail of his very bold plan.

*   *   *

On the other side of the country, Dino was listening to Monarch's elevation of Tobey to one of the best drivers in America. And though he wasn't showing it, he was furious.

He was sitting inside the office of his company's new customizing garage in California. The place was state-of-the-art and, of course, it was enormous. It had twelve lifts, banks of the latest diagnostic equipment, and top-of-the-line computers everywhere. The tools alone cost several hundred thousand dollars. Yet the floor was waxed and so clean you could eat off of it. The place looked more like his dealership's showroom next door than a customizing shop. The sign above the door identified it as Dino Brewster Motors.

The office itself was as well-organized as the workshop beyond, but with a lot more good taste. This was evidence that Anita had had a hand in its design.

She was sitting across from Dino at the moment, watching the footage Monarch was displaying and following along on her laptop.

The podcast host raged on, "My people, reigning De Leon champ Dino Brewster is on the line with us right now. Dino Dino Bambino—Fee Fi Fofino—you need to see what I'm seeing. It's aerial footage, my man! I don't know who's shooting it, but Tobey Marshall is flying across the country right now, cops in tow, in a phantom Ford that would make your bowels loose."

Dino just laughed.

"So Tobey Marshall is doing something stupid again?" he asked. "Is that what you're saying? Did we all forget that this is the guy who just got out of prison for manslaughter?"

Monarch replied: "Accidents happen in racing, Dino Dino Bambino. And that car he's driving is one of a kind."

"I know it's one of a kind," Dino said defiantly. "Because I'm the one who put that car in Tobey's hands."

The Mustang was still tearing down Highway 12 at that moment. Its current speed was near 120 mph and climbing.

Tobey and Julia were closely following Monarch's conversation with Dino.

Tobey in particular was taking it all in, staring straight ahead— but increasing his speed to more aggressive limits. It didn't take a shrink to tell that Dino's comments were having an effect on him.

Suddenly, Julia spotted two cars up ahead, driving side by side, taking up both lanes of the highway. She sensed a problem right away.

"Lane four," she said simply.

But Tobey didn't respond. He was still accelerating— and getting closer to the pair of dawdling cars.

"Lane one?" she asked.

Still, Tobey stayed mute. Monarch's show was continuing, providing a strange soundtrack for the suddenly growing drama inside the Mustang.

Dino's voice fell out of the speaker again.

"Tobey Marshall is simply reckless behind the wheel," he said in no uncertain terms. "That's just about the only thing he's famous for."

As if to prove Dino's point, Tobey refused to change lanes. Instead he punched the gas pedal, accelerated tremendously and split the two slower cars at an ungodly speed.

Julia was getting used to this sort of thing by now. Still, she said to him, "Do you know a fully loaded commercial airliner takes flight at a hundred seventy miles an hour?"

Tobey seemed unimpressed. Dino's words were still burning in his ears.

"So?" he replied.

"So, we're just doing one eighty-five," she said, pointing to the speedometer. "Just thought you'd enjoy that fun fact."

Meanwhile, Monarch was having a hard time believing what Dino was trying to sell.

"*You're* worried about reckless driving?" he asked Dino directly. "*You?* The same Dino Bambino who got thrown out of Indy for wrecking guys under a caution flag? Methinks you protest too much, Fee-Fi-Fofino."

What Dino said next shocked Monarch's audience, including Tobey and Julia.

"If that's his plan, I don't want to see Tobey Marshall at the De Leon," Dino said emphatically. "Matter of fact, I'm willing to give my Lambo Elemento away to anyone who can stop him."

Monarch cut in. "Now, wait a second, Dino," he said. "I know you're rich. But that's insane. You're willing to give someone your Elemento? That car is one of three in the world. You're just going to *give* it to anybody who stops Tobey Marshall? Do you realize that means you'll also lose your place in this year's race?"

Anita was staring intently at Dino as he was going back and forth with Monarch. She was supremely puzzled and shocked at her boyfriend's bizarre offer.

Why would Dino want to give up his spot in the De Leon just to stop Tobey?

At that moment, Dino glanced out his office window and into his shop beyond. Two men in suits had just entered the garage.

They looked like they were right out of a mobster movie. One of them was Paul "Pauly Nuts" Lawrence. He was the "other" investor that Dino had mentioned at dinner not long before. Lawrence was talking to Big Al, Dino's obese and sweaty garage manager.

After a brief conversation, Big Al headed toward Dino's office, obviously bearing some kind of message.

Dino stood up immediately, his inflammatory conversation with Monarch forgotten for the moment. He knew these guys needed his immediate attention.

Anita had spotted them, too. She studied them through the office window as Big Al came in.

Dino held up his hand—a signal for Big Al to keep his mouth shut for the moment.

He got back to Monarch.

"Yes, that's right," Dino said. "I'm posting a picture of that Mustang now, so everyone knows what they're looking for. Consider it a bounty on Tobey Marshall's head."

With that, Dino hit upload, then walked out from behind his desk to talk to Big Al.

"That douche bag out there wants to talk to you," Big Al told Dino.

But Anita wanted to talk to Dino first.

"You realize you just put a three-million-dollar bounty on Tobey, don't you?" she asked in disbelief. "Why are you doing this?"

"He killed your brother, Anita," Dino replied harshly. "I'm doing this for *you*."

Anita was so floored by this response, she couldn't speak for a moment. But Dino didn't notice. He was too focused on the men in suits.

He put on his best charming face, then walked out into the garage to meet them.

Back on Highway 12, Tobey and Julia were still glued to Monarch's show, hanging on his every word.

"Oh, the drama!" Monarch bellowed. "I've got star-crossed lovers doing one fifty across the country."

"Make that one eighty," Julia interjected.

"And now," Monarch went on, "the reigning De Leon Champ—Dino Brewster—just painted a huge bull's-eye on their backs!"

Julia took a moment to look over at Tobey. But he was still expressionless and staring straight ahead.

Monarch was going nonstop. "Yes, Christmas came to us early, my little wing nuts!" he said with a laugh. "Racing is art . . . but racing with passion is high art!

"I can feel love and vengeance and motor oil swirling together out there! You heard it and it bears repeating! Dino Brewster is offering a Lamborghini Elemento to anyone who brings him that Mustang. And my math says that incredible car just left Michigan. This Tobey Marshall is a marked man! We've got supernatural Mustangs and personal vendettas—I have no idea what's going on out there, but I know *I love it*!"

On a particularly empty stretch of Highway 12, a Michigan state trooper was driving east. The Shelby Mustang was still heading west on the other side of the divided highway.

The trooper saw the supercar coming and his dash radar was already activated. But strangely, no miles per hour number showed up on his screen.

It was like the Mustang was invisible—and, in a way, it was. Julia was negating the cop's radar with the laser jammer, turning the Mustang into a true stealth.

Once by the cop, Julia synced into Monarch's stream.

"Monarch?" she spoke into the mic. "This is the blonde female sitting right next to Tobey Marshall."

Monarch was immediately delighted.

"On the air right now is a blonde bird from Britain," he announced. He quickly switched to a bad British accent: "Pip, pip, cheerio, little bird who claims to be sitting next to Tobey Marshall in that Mustang. Having tea are you, love?"

But Tobey was less than thrilled that Julia had opened a link to Monarch.

"Can you pay attention?" he asked her. "I need you."

Julia was all but ignoring him, though.

"No," she replied.

At that moment, Tobey spotted a truck dead ahead. He applied the brakes and downshifted. Smoothly moving across the highway lanes, he was soon driving on the shoulder, where he upshifted and accelerated past the truck like it was standing still.

Just beyond, he spotted a sign welcoming them to Indiana.

Beyond that was an on-ramp for Interstate I-80 West.

With the flick of his wrist, Tobey jumped on the on-ramp at 160 mph. Seconds later he was on I-80 West itself. Finally, they were back on the interstate, where they belonged.

Julia, meanwhile, was still on the line to Monarch's show.

"There were three cars in that race the night that kid Little Pete died," she told him and his audience. "That is a *fact*. And for anyone who believes that Tobey was responsible for the death of Pete—well, ask yourself this: Why would he jump parole in New York, knowing he could get rearrested and do serious time, unless he is innocent and hellbent on righting a wrong? He did his time, paid his debt. So why would he risk it? When you talk to Dino again, you should ask him."

There was a long moment of silence.

Then Tobey said to her, "Thank you."

"You're welcome," she replied.

Another moment of silence.

Then Monarch came on again.

"Well, I'm moved," he said. "This might be a first for me. My heart of stone just softened."

Then Monarch launched into his bad British accent again.

"I believe you," he said. "You crazed little tart. I think you're bloody serious . . . I really do."

Monarch switched back to his normal voice.

"And I hear you," he went on. "And I know that the two of you are flying across the country at killer speeds to prove something . . . Sounds like a deep rivalry, Tobey Marshall versus Dino Brewster—I ain't got a dog in this fight, but I flat-out *love* the fight! Born to run baby, you two kids tearing up the American asphalt!"

Monarch stopped for another moment; he was thinking.

"You know what?" he went on again. "Tell Tobey Marshall I say . . . welcome to De Leon. Tobey, old boy, if you can get here in one piece, I'm happy to have you on the line with us. I have spoken. Good night, little bird. Pleasant dreams . . ."

* * *

Among the many listening to Monarch's show was the street racer known as the Flyin' Hawaiian.

He was a large, brutish man with long greasy hair braided into long pigtails. He was in his shop near LA working on his 4x4 pre-runner. These kinds of vehicles had gotten their start when people began modifying simple Toyota two-wheel-drive trucks to run in off-road races, usually through the desert. The idea grew until just about any small truck with big wheels and off-road modifications was called a pre-runner.

The Hawaiian was watching Monarch's broadcast on a flat screen TV mounted to the wall of his less-than-organized garage. It was the opposite of Dino's place: messy, smelly, full of parts scattered everywhere.

The place fit its owner. Drinking a beer and smoking a blunt, the Flyin' Hawaiian was enthralled by what Monarch was saying. He was, in some ways, the anti-Tobey. He'd done time in prison—for assault—but he had been the head of a gang who beat up new meat. He'd dealt drugs, chopped stolen cars, and even sold illegal guns in Mexico—his conscience had never been his guide. He was the ultimate bully, but also the ultimate coward. Never known for taking on an opponent mano a mano, he'd never fought a fair fight in his life. And he wasn't about to start anytime soon.

"And that's it, my people," Monarch said, wrapping up his show. "The De Leon is full. But Dino Brewster's

Lambo Elemento is still in play. And that means his spot in the race is also up for grabs.

"If you want it, you're gonna have to chase down that Super Mustang to get it. It's the race before the race . . ."

Monarch's final words of the evening were for the passengers of the Super Mustang.

"And this is for Tobey Marshall," he concluded. "I will text you the exact details for the meeting place for the De Leon. But remember—this requires honor among thieves! No snitching! Until then, run, Tobey, run!"

No sooner had Monarch signed off than Benny was on the radio. The Mustang was roaring along I-80 at 150 mph. The sun was setting in front of them.

"Beauty," Benny began. "I've been listening in. Congrats on the wild card ticket to the rodeo. Your route is clear to the Nebraska border. Darkness is upon us, so the eyes in the sky will be shut down for a while. I'm going to leapfrog ahead and meet you at the record breaker."

"Okay, roger that," Tobey replied. "And thanks."

Back in Dino's office Anita closed her laptop as soon as Monarch's show ended.

She continued watching Dino and the mysterious men in suits out in the garage. She thought a moment, then got up and went around to Dino's desk.

She sat down at his laptop and started punching keys. She quickly became lost in what she was reading . . .

Suddenly a voice interrupted her. "What are you doing?"

She looked up to see Dino reach across the desk and slowly close his laptop. Just the way he did this concerned her. There was something threatening about it.

"I'm just working," she answered, though a bit unsteadily.

Dino's expression turned very sinister at her reply.

But he said no more.

Eighteen

IT WAS A small victory when the Mustang crossed the state line into Nebraska.

Not only did Tobey feel good about leaving Michigan and Indiana behind—not to mention Illinois and Iowa. But in his mind, making Nebraska meant they were halfway to their goal of California. In other words, it was all downhill from here.

Shortly into the Cornhusker state, a large neon sign announced an upcoming truck stop.

It was late at night by now; they'd been driving virtually nonstop. It was time for a break.

Tobey pulled into the rest stop, reducing his speed drastically in order to make the entranceway.

The place was full of fuel pumps for both trucks and cars, plus a diner and a Quik Mart. It was for good reason this rest stop was open twenty-four hours a day. There were people moving about and a fair amount of activity.

Tobey brought the Mustang to a stop and jumped out. He stretched mightily and started pumping high-grade into the Mustang's nearly depleted gas tank. Meanwhile, Julia headed for the bathroom.

"Please hustle," Tobey called after her. "We're two hours behind schedule. And, by the way, keep it low-key. Monarch just made you famous. Okay?"

"Got it," Julia replied, jogging to the Quik Mart. "Trust me—I'll be fast."

The refueling went quickly. But just as Tobey finished up, a Nebraska State Police patrol car pulled into the truck stop. Tobey coolly ducked down, then scurried to the cover of a pickup truck parked in the adjacent gas bay.

Once hidden, he pulled out his cell phone while slowly sliding his way up the outer wall of the pickup's bed.

But it was only when he peeked into the truck's bed that he realized a huge dog was waiting there, attached to a chain.

The animal lunged at him, snarling, teeth bared and barking loudly. The commotion was loud enough to attract the attention of the state trooper.

The trooper stopped and looked in the dog's direction. He thought a moment, contemplating whether he should walk over to the pickup. But after seeing the dog was chained, he decided against it. He headed into the truck stop instead.

At the same moment, Julia walked out of the restroom,

where she had just changed her clothes. She was casually spritzing some expensive perfume on as she headed for the front door.

That's when she spotted the trooper. She calmly slowed her gait, redirecting her path to an aisle farther away from him.

Working behind the cash register was a bored teenage waitress blowing bubbles with her chewing gum.

The trooper walked up to her and said two words: "Coffee, black."

By force of habit, the trooper casually looked up at the truck stop's security monitor, hanging over the cash register. All eight of the video feeds were displaying the gas pumps.

Glittering like some gigantic jewel on wheels, the Silver Mustang was front and center on one of the TV monitors.

The trooper quickly changed his order. "Make that to go," he told the waitress.

At that moment, Julia's cell phone began ringing. Not only was it turned on loud but it was blaring the very familiar Michael Jackson "Beat It" ringtone.

The trooper turned toward the sound.

Meanwhile, Julia had ducked behind a candy rack. She answered the phone.

It was Tobey.

"Hey, yes, I know," Julia said, whispering into the phone.

But then she got the feeling someone was in back of her.

She turned around to find the trooper standing right behind her.

"Excuse me, miss?" he said to her. "Can I ask you a few questions?"

Julia slipped the phone into her handbag without disconnecting and then stood up.

"Why, of course, you can," she replied, trying hard to affect a southern accent.

She read his badge.

"Officer Lejeune," she added. "How can I help you?"

"Do you live in the area?" the trooper asked her.

She shook her head. "No, sir," she replied. "We're long haulin'."

The trooper studied her outfit and thought about her accent.

"Is that right?" he asked, skeptically.

Julia laughed, though she was fighting mightily to stay calm.

"Yes, sir," she replied.

Meanwhile, Tobey had quietly walked around the trooper's car. He was now peering through the store's windows to see what was going on.

Inside, he could see the trooper was studying Julia up and down as she was spinning her yarn.

"You're not traveling in that silver Mustang out there?" the trooper asked her.

"Mustang?" she replied. "No, sir."

Julia took a step toward the front door, but the trooper blocked her path.

"I'd like to ask you a few more questions," the trooper told her. "If you'd step out to my cruiser—it shouldn't take but a minute."

Julia froze. She was certain the jig was up. The trooper walked to the front door and held it open for her. She followed him, but just for one step. Then she turned around and bolted toward the back of the store, running as fast as she could.

The trooper was stunned, but only for a moment. He took off after her in a snap, chasing her down a hallway.

Outside, Tobey was hustling back to the Mustang. He was still trying to look inside the store, all the while listening to Julia on his phone.

Her voice came on in a shrill whisper. "Tobey! There's a cop in here!"

"I know," Tobey told her. "Where are you?"

At that moment, Julia was running frantically down the hallway, the trooper right on her heels.

The hallway ended at a staircase. Julia ran up the stairs, but the trooper was gaining on her.

She reached the top of the stairs and ran through an open doorway, slamming the door behind her and locking it.

"I'm upstairs now!" she yelled to Tobey over the phone. "I'm in a room! Like a storage room."

"Is there a window?" Tobey asked her quickly.

Julia ran to the room's only window. Suddenly the trooper was banging mightily on the locked door.

"Yes, there's a window," she told Tobey. "But I'm on the second floor!"

Tobey could hear the trooper yelling in the background, "I'm asking you to open this door, miss!"

"Climb out the window," Tobey urged Julia. "I'll be there."

Julia never stopped moving. She climbed atop some boxes as quickly as she could, trying to get out the window.

The trooper was pounding on the door with his billy club now. His voice was insistent.

"Miss, you need to open this door, *right now*!"

Then he clicked on his walkie-talkie.

"This is Unit Seven Two," he barked into it. "I'm at the truck stop on Eighty. Any units in the area? Over."

In this short amount of time, Julia had managed to crawl halfway out the window. With one last push, she popped onto the roof.

But then she peeked over the edge and saw it was about a fifteen-foot drop to the ground.

"Oh damn!" she growled to herself. "Damn, I don't like this."

She looked in every direction—but Tobey was nowhere in sight.

She began running along the roof, frantically looking down into the parking lot while yelling into her phone.

"Tobey—come and get me!" she screamed. "I'm up on the roof!"

An instant later, the Mustang appeared right below her.

Tobey called out the car's window, "You gotta jump. Let's go!"

But there was a problem.

"I'm afraid of heights," she yelled back down to him. "I can't even bear to look down!"

"It's not that high!" he called back up to her. "Just jump!"

"I can't!" she bellowed back. "I'm *terrified* of heights."

Tobey got out of the Mustang and ran to a point right below Julia.

"Sit on the edge!" he called up to her. "Hang your feet over. I'll catch you."

But Julia was having none of that. She was stamping her feet in furious fear.

"Shit . . . Shit . . . *Shit!*" she yelled, mad at herself and her phobia. But there was nowhere else she could go, nothing else she could do.

So she finally crept to the edge of the roof and let her feet dangle over.

"Now close your eyes and just jump!" Tobey yelled up to her. "On three . . . One . . ."

Julia closed her eyes and jumped—a full two seconds too early. Tobey was not ready—but he caught her anyway. Absorbing the impact with his prison-built muscles, he spun them both against the car and then softly to the ground.

Tobey recovered quickly, picked up Julia, and practically threw her into the Mustang. Then he jumped in and floored it. The Mustang rocketed away in a cloud of smoke and dust.

By this time, the trooper had run out of the store. He was still barking into his walkie-talkie.

"In pursuit of the silver Mustang!" he reported to his

headquarters. "New York plates . . . Going back to my cruiser now!"

The trooper jumped into his cruiser and fired up the engine. He put it in gear and punched the gas pedal. The car lurched forward—but only for a couple feet. Then it began bucking wildly from behind. Suddenly there was a great *crash!* The cruiser's rear axle smashed into the asphalt while the rest of the car kept going. It finally ground to a halt after twenty feet or so.

The trooper quickly recovered from the shock and looked in his rearview mirror. That's when he realized the axle had been tethered with a thick chain to a large semitruck parked in front of the store.

The trooper just shook his head. His car was toast, and he knew it.

Then he heard another noise.

He looked over at the pickup truck he'd seen before to see the huge, now-unchained dog barking at him maniacally.

Not a minute later, Tobey and Julia were roaring down the highway again. She kept looking in her side mirror, expecting to see police lights at any moment.

Just seconds after their getaway, the iPad crackled to life. It contained a text from Monarch.

It read, "The drivers' meeting is at 8:00 p.m. at the Intercontinental Hotel in Frisco. Be there square or you will not get the actual location of the race."

Tobey looked over at Julia, who was still catching her breath from their escape. She had changed into clothes he was more used to—jeans and a T-shirt. But more important, he'd just seen a side of her that he never knew existed.

He was wearing a wide smile. He was really beginning to respect her—and more.

But she was still worried about the cop.

"Where is he?" she asked Tobey, continuing to check in the mirrors.

"He's not coming," he replied confidently.

"Really?" she asked. It was almost like she didn't want to believe it.

"Trust me," Tobey replied. "He'll be stuck back there for a while."

"Are you sure?" she asked, needing confirmation.

Tobey laughed to himself; one word came to mind: *Chains* . . .

"Oh, yeah," he said. "I'm sure."

Suddenly, Joe Peck's voice crackled through the Mustang.

"Beauty?" he began. "I'm listening to the trooper chatter and it sounds like your princess got snagged."

"Yeah, it was rough back there," Tobey replied with a smirk.

"Well, we couldn't have planned it any better," Joe told him. "You're solo now and lighter by 100 pounds."

Tobey looked at Julia.

"Maybe 105 . . ." he told Joe. "Or more . . ."

Julia whacked him good-naturedly.

"I pity the cops who have to listen to her go on and on," Tobey added. "That girl just does not shut up. *Ever . . .*"

"I copy that, homeboy," Joe replied.

"I'm kidding," Tobey finally revealed. "I still got her. It was like a scene from *The Great Escape . . .* over."

Joe immediately tried to redeem himself.

"I've always liked you, Julia," he said half seriously. "You know that."

"Thanks, Joe," she said. "Over and out."

With that, Julia flipped a switch, effectively ending the conversation.

"You *were* impressive back there," Tobey told her, now that they were finally alone. "It makes me wonder if you could maybe drive for a few hours?"

Julia nodded happily. "For sure!" she exclaimed. "But do you really think we should stop?"

Tobey didn't reply. Instead, he grabbed her hand and pulled her into his lap. Then he put her hands on the steering wheel, and after enjoying her perfume a little more than he should have, slid over into the passenger's seat.

"The con is yours, my dear," he told her. "And in case you forgot—we're going to San Francisco."

She gave him a mock salute, still a little flustered that their bodies had been entangled for those quick few seconds. She had no complaints, though.

"Aye, aye, Captain," she said. "Next stop—Frisco!"

Nineteen

THE SUNRISE OVER the Utah mountains was like something from a postcard.

Julia was still driving; Tobey had fallen asleep a long time ago. All was quiet inside the Mustang. No iPhone chat. No police scanner. No Monarch.

Julia felt good—and was feeling fully confident behind the wheel of the supercar.

Until disaster struck.

One moment she was driving along in high-speed contentment; the next, the Mustang was hit violently from behind.

The supercar went sideways from the impact. Julia saw that a huge Hummer-like vehicle had come up behind them and she knew instinctively it was the Flyin' Hawaiian. But she was terrified to see his right-seater hanging out the window, aiming a shotgun at her.

Tobey woke up in an instant. The Mustang was out of control, and Julia was screaming.

"*Jesus!*" she bellowed. "That was *on purpose*!"

Tobey realized what was happening in a microsecond.

He yelled, "Yeah—thanks to Dino's bounty!"

Julia regained control of the car, but suddenly, a glossy chrome Hummer and a muddy Bronco appeared from the opposite direction. He was never one to fight fairly—the Flyin' Hawaiian and his goons were trying to trap them.

"They're going to seal us off!" Tobey yelled to Julia. "Drift onto the shoulder."

"Nope," she said to his surprise. "I've got a better idea."

"And that is?" he yelled at her.

"I'm going for the Hummer," she said. "He's a pavement prowler."

Tobey was confused. "Pavement prowler?" he repeated loudly.

"Show car with a big lift kit," Julia yelled back. "Helps make up for the inferiority complex."

Julia held out her pinky finger and let it droop—Tobey got the idea. Small package. Frightened turtle.

She hit the gas hard, accelerating mightily toward the oncoming vehicles. In an instant, she swerved into the wrong lane, aiming right for the Hummer. It was a game of chicken. A very deadly one. Tobey grabbed the dash and door, holding on for dear life, just as Julia had done so many times earlier in the trip.

He heard his own voice screaming, "Are you *crazy?*"

But Julia didn't lift her foot off the gas. She kept driving right at the Hummer. Only at the last possible instant did the big truck swerve to miss her. But in doing so, it piled up on the highway's median, hitting a rock wall head on. The impact caused the big truck to flip, end over end in midair. Julia simply drove under the airborne wreck and kept right on going.

This got Tobey's heart rate pumping, maybe like never before.

"Wow—you *are* crazy!" he yelled.

Julia looked over at him and smiled. Her expression said it all. She was quite impressed with herself.

Then came the shotgun blast.

Tobey heard it clearly above all the commotion and the roar of his Mustang's mighty engine.

He turned to see the Flyin' Hawaiian's Baja pre-runner right on their tail. His right-seater was leaning out the window, an enormous twelve-gauge in hand. A second later he fired another shotgun blast.

The back window of the Mustang exploded in a shower of sparks and glass. Both Julia and Tobey ducked just in time to avoid getting hit by the flying shards. But the Mustang was suddenly swerving uncontrollably.

"Keep it straight!" he yelled to Julia.

"I'm trying!" she yelled back.

Tobey looked out the newly windowless back and saw

that the Flyin' Hawaiian was on the radio even as he was bearing down on the Mustang. His right-seater was back out the window, aiming another shotgun blast. This time it seemed the Mustang's rear tires were his targets.

Suddenly Julia was urgently tapping Tobey's shoulder. He looked straight ahead and saw two cement trucks driving at full throttle, coming down the highway, aiming right at the Mustang.

Tobey quickly grabbed his radio.

"Liar One!" he yelled for Benny. "You got your ears on?"

Then Tobey saw a dirt road off to the left. It was coming up fast.

He yelled to Julia, "Take your foot off the gas when I say so—and then go hard left, okay?"

"Okay," Julia said, concentrating as best she could.

"Your instinct is going to be to let go," Tobey warned her.

"Just do it!" she yelled back at him.

Tobey yanked up on the emergency brake and Julia took the hard left. Amid the smoke from the tires and exhaust, the Mustang drifted perfectly onto the dirt road.

But the Flyin' Hawaiian followed—and was suddenly driving with even more confidence than before. In his mind, the Mustang had just taken his bait—and fallen into his trap.

There was a fork in the road up ahead and the Bronco took it, disappearing from view. The Mustang continued on the side road and began climbing up the side of a mountain, going through a series of hard lefts and rights—all at extremely high speed.

But then they came to a scary hairpin turn. Julia was trying her best, but she turned too quickly, and then tried to overcompensate, almost bouncing the car off the cliff wall.

What she lacked in skill, though, she made up for with pure aggression.

"Dammit!" she yelled. "I should be better at this!"

"Don't let up!" Tobey yelled back at her. "You're doing good!"

Julia took his advice and stood on the gas pedal.

Nearby, but out of their sight, the Ford Bronco was blasting up a parallel dirt road. It was rough, but the truck's suspension was more than a match for it. In fact, it was actually gathering speed as it went uphill.

At the same time, the Flyin' Hawaiian was right behind the Mustang and gaining on them. His right-seater fired another shotgun blast. This one hit off a huge boulder right in front of the supercar, showering it with rock fragments.

The Hawaiian's right-seater was being bounced around a lot as he tried to reload. As a result, most of his shotgun shells had fallen to the floor of the Baja.

Still, the Flyin' Hawaiian was just a few feet off the Shelby's bumper.

The mad chase continued, the Mustang going extremely fast, kicking up dirt and gravel, the Baja getting closer by the second. Then the road abruptly turned from a two-track dirt path to almost no road at all. Suddenly the Mustang was going over some very rough ground—not its best trait.

Tobey searched a map on his iPad. "We've got to find another road!" he yelled to Julia.

"Up here?" Julia yelled back. "There's only one road—or there was . . ."

Tobey grabbed the radio and starting shouting into it again. "Liar One—Liar One! We need you."

The Flyin' Hawaiian was right on the Mustang's ass now—just inches away. This kind of driving is what he had built his truck for: spitting dirt and rock, all four barrels wide open. As they raced up the side of the mountain at breakneck speed, the truck was gaining on the Mustang with every second.

The biggest problem was, the Mustang was not built for off-roading, and its undercarriage was seriously bottoming out. Julia was driving as fast as she could without tearing the wheels off the car, but it was no use. They were nearing the summit of the mountain, and their pursuers would be on them in seconds.

But then came . . . a miracle of sorts.

And it was all thanks to an angel named Benny.

Suddenly the Mustang's windshield was filled with the sight of an enormous CH-53 Super Stallion helicopter. The gigantic aircraft rose above the Mustang and floated to a position right over it.

Tobey was immediately on the radio.

"Liar One?" he yelled. "Is that you?"

Suddenly, drop lines from the helicopter fell to the ground and dragged along both sides of the supercar.

Then Tobey and Julia heard Benny's voice fill the car.

"Hook up!" he was yelling. "Hurry!"

Benny was in the copilot's seat of the massive U.S. Army chopper. An army pilot was in the seat next to him.

"Sergeant!," the man was yelling at Benny now, "this is *not* what we discussed."

"It will be fine, sir," Benny told him. "Don't worry."

Still driving as fast as they could, Tobey and Julia ran the helicopter's lift hooks through the open windows of the Mustang. Then Tobey connected them together inside.

Benny's voice came over the radio again.

"Tell me you believe I can fly an Apache helicopter," he yelled at Tobey.

Tobey couldn't believe what he was hearing.

"*What?*" was all he could reply.

The Mustang and the Super Stallion helicopter were now hooked together, attached by the drop lines. Suddenly, up ahead, Tobey and Julia could see the Bronco coming right at them. A collision was imminent.

But Benny wasn't lifting them yet.

"I'm serious," he called down to Tobey. "Tell me."

Julia yelled at Tobey, "Say whatever he wants!"

Tobey relented quickly. He yelled into the microphone, "Okay, you can fly an Apache helicopter!"

"And my handle is Maverick," Benny responded. "Call me Maverick."

"Okay," Tobey yelled back. "You're Maverick—you're a fucking maverick!"

They could hear Benny laughing over the radio speaker.

"Now was that so hard?" he asked.

The Bronco was seconds from penning them off with the Flyin' Hawaiian still glued to their rear. But the edge of the cliff was also coming up fast.

Julia had no other choice. She drove the Mustang off the cliff . . .

And at that very instant, the Super Stallion's straps went taut, catching the supercar and suspending it underneath.

Tobey and Julia couldn't believe what was happening.

"Holy shit!" she yelled. "This is crazy!"

The Flyin' Hawaiian and his right-seater watched in disbelief as the enormous helicopter flew the Mustang up and out of their grasp.

But there was one problem. The Mustang was hanging almost straight down over the vast gorge below. The bottom of the gorge suddenly filled their windshield. Julia and Tobey were pointing straight down even as the helicopter began to gain altitude.

But because Julia was terrified of heights, this was her worst nightmare.

"Oh my god!" she screamed again. *"Oh my god!"*

She was so terrified that she was holding her breath, which was turning her face beet-red. She was freaking out and trying to cry, but she couldn't because she had no air.

Tobey grabbed her by the shoulders.

"Julia—look at me!" he yelled.

She did as he asked, but was still red in the face and still not breathing.

"Focus on my eyes," he told her. "Now . . . breathe, Julia. *Breathe!*"

Julia exhaled and started gasping—but it was a start. Tobey continued to soothe her.

"Good," he said. "Now breathe . . . relax . . . and focus on my eyes. What color are they?"

"Blue," Julia managed to reply. "They're *really* blue . . ."

"A little bluer than yours," Tobey told her.

"No, they're not," she said. And for one fleeting and crazy moment, they were lost in each other's eyes.

Then finally, Julia smiled broadly. She was breathing again. Tobey had successfully talked her down.

At that moment, the huge helicopter banked to the left and flew on, the Mustang hanging safely below.

Twenty

▮▮▮▮▮▬▬▬▬▬▬▬▬▬

EVERY RACING CAR enthusiast in the world knew about the Bonneville Salt Flats.

A giant, flat piece of desert located in northwest Utah, it was, in reality, a gigantic dry lake bed, surrounded on all sides by picture-perfect mountains.

This was the place where many race car records had been broken over the years, and where many experimental cars and motorcycles had been tested.

Sitting here now was the Beast, with Joe Peck and Finn lounging in the back, waiting for the prearranged meet-up with the Mustang.

Suddenly, they were aware of something flying over the mountains and heading right for them. They stared at it silently for a long time.

"Is that our car?" Finn finally gasped.

"Under a helicopter?" Joe added.

It was the Mustang and it *was* being carried by an enormous helicopter.

But they couldn't believe what they were seeing.

"Do they put something in the water out here?" Finn asked. "Mormon acid or something?"

The helicopter went into a hover right above them. The downwash from its blades kicked up a blizzard of white dust and salt. But still, Joe and Finn could see that while it was the Mustang, its undercarriage was heavily damaged.

The car was slowly lowered to the ground. The front end touched first, fairly gently. But then the back end came down hard, crashing to the ground like a heap of junk.

The car was immediately detached from the copter's cables. Suddenly the doors opened and Tobey and Julia emerged from the mangled racer. Joe Peck and Finn ran over to them, still fighting the copter's massive downwash.

"Jessuz!" Joe Peck exclaimed. "What the hell happened? Are you guys okay?"

They both answered at once. Tobey said, "Yes," while Julia replied with a resounding *"No!"*

Meanwhile, the huge copter rose in altitude, with its hook cables dangling. Then, from another direction, came another thunderous noise. It dwarfed any racket that the Shelby had ever made.

Suddenly two F-16 fighter planes roared overhead. The four of them watched in awe as the two jets screamed by.

"Something tells me they want their helicopter back," Julia said, looking up at the fierce warplanes.

The Beast's radio came to life. A very authoritative voice boomed: "One Alpha Bravo Victor Charlie—this is the United States Army."

Then they heard Benny's voice. "Hope everyone is okay down there," he said. "I might have to go away for a bit."

They all watched as the helicopter turned east and sank behind some hills.

"Godspeed, boys," they heard Benny say before the copter disappeared for good.

Suddenly, they were all alone out on the expansive salt flats. The wind was blowing, but everything else was quiet. No one said anything for a few moments. It had been a strange turn of events, to say the least.

Finally Tobey told them a quick version of the story and then nodded toward the banged-up Mustang. He looked at Joe as if to say, "What do you think?"

Joe just laughed.

"Yeah, we can make her run again," he said. "But . . ."

"Just do your best," Tobey told him.

Joe and Finn didn't move, though. They had to have a serious talk with Tobey.

"We heard about your cop friend getting chained back in Nebraska," Joe told him.

"And Benny is going to be in the brig in about ten minutes," Finn said.

"Plus, there's an APB out for your arrest in at least ten states right now," Joe added.

Tobey just shrugged. "So what's your point?" he asked them.

"Maybe we should rethink the plan," Joe finally suggested.

Tobey just stared back at his two friends.

"Dino took everything from me," he said to them. "From us. Including Pete. Pete got put in the ground and Dino went to sunny California like nothing happened."

A long pause ensued. The wind was blowing fiercely across the flats. No one said a word.

"You guys do what you think is right," Tobey finally told them. "But I'm never going to stop."

**Part
Six**

Twenty-One

IT WAS MIDAFTERNOON when the Mustang blew past a sign that read, "Welcome to Nevada."

The car was a mess. The undercarriage was in shambles. The body had dents galore. It was dirty and dusty all over, especially the remaining windows, which were coated with some kind of greasy slime.

But it could still move very fast, and at that moment Tobey had the accelerator buried.

Julia was back in the right seat. She'd been pensive since they'd left the salt flats.

"What are you thinking about?" she finally asked Tobey.

"That I never should've made that deal with Dino," he replied.

The expression on his face told the tale. Dealing with Dino had been akin to dealing with the devil.

"You needed the money, though," Julia told him. "Nothing wrong with that."

"My father would have never done it," Tobey replied sternly.

Julia let that comment sit for a while.

"Is your mom still alive?" she asked him quietly.

"No," he replied.

"That's too bad," Julia said. "What was she like?"

"She was beautiful," he replied wistfully. "In fact, before she met my dad, she used to model, for calendars— tasteful ones. The kind they'd hang up in repair garages and gas stations way back when. She could have gone to New York and done some real modeling, but she chose to get married and start a family instead."

"That must have been a big decision for her," Julia said. "Do you think it worked out the way she wanted it to?"

"I think so," he replied. "I mean, when I was a real little kid I remember that she was always smiling, always a big smile on her face whenever I looked up at her. It was the same way when I was growing up. I loved driving on the go-cart track and then, later, the shifter cars. She'd always be there to watch me—her and my dad. And I'd go around the course a few dozen times, and she was always just standing there, not rooting me on as much as just smiling at me every time I went by."

"She died when you were young, I take it?" Julia asked.

"Yeah, when I was eleven," Tobey replied quietly. "I was

too dorky to figure out what was going on until it was too late. Just a lot of doctors' visits, at odd times of day— sometimes early in the morning. Sometimes in the middle of the night. But she was always there when I woke up in the morning, always had my breakfast ready. It all seemed really strange at the time.

"Then came the trips to the hospital, again at weird hours, and after that she wasn't always there to make my breakfast in the morning.

"Then one day, I was coming home from school and I saw her being put into an ambulance. And I saw my father crying—the one and only time for that. She held my hand for a moment, and she never stopped smiling. Then the ambulance took off, siren, lights flashing, the whole bit. But I never saw her alive again."

Julia's breath caught in her throat. "That's heartbreaking, Tobey," she said.

He just shrugged. "Everyone has to go through it eventually, right?" he said. "It's just that I was still a kid—and my father was just never the same afterward. I feel like we grew old together, just the two of us, in a big empty house. Then one day at work, he was under a car, changing an oil line, and he had a heart attack. He was dead before the EMTs got there, even before I could call 911. Peck was there when it happened. I'd never seen Peck cry, either, until that day."

Julia was on the verge of tears herself. She touched his arm, lightly and only for a moment.

"They sound like good people," she told him. "Your

father, solid, hardworking. Your mom, beautiful—you made her happy. That's why she was always smiling."

"She *was* beautiful," Tobey said again, after taking a deep breath. Then he looked right at Julia and added, "And while I'm not the smartest guy in the world, I do know a beautiful woman when I see one."

Several hundred miles to the west, Dino and Anita were in his 2012 Ferrari Berlinetta, driving through the streets of San Francisco.

Dino was at the wheel and on the phone. He was all but ignoring Anita.

They arrived at a very exclusive restaurant, pulling up out front with a screech. Only then did Dino hang up the phone.

"Dammit!" he cursed.

"How much do you owe him?" Anita asked him. "Or should I ask, at what point will they actually break your kneecaps?"

Dino paid her no mind, but she decided to press him.

"Those two goons who came to the shop yesterday," she said. "They work for him, don't they?"

Dino just looked at her with very hard eyes, but still remained silent.

"How did it happen?" she asked. "How did you get in so deep with these mobsters?"

"It's none of your business," Dino said. He was growing angry. "Just stay out of it."

"No, I won't," she shot back at him. "I can't."

"Look, I'm taking care of it," he said sternly.

But she would not let up.

"Why is Tobey risking everything to race you?" she asked him. "He has so much to lose if he's caught. So much to lose even if he isn't. It makes no sense . . . unless—"

"Watch yourself," Dino warned her darkly.

At that moment, the restaurant's valet, Juan, tried to open the Ferrari's door, but Dino had locked it. He tapped on the window as another car pulled up in back of the mega-expensive sports car.

Dino cracked the window and said, "Hey, Paco—you touch this car again and you're screwed. You understand?"

With that, Dino rolled the window back up.

In the next moment, Juan, a few more valets, and some passing customers witnessed a shocking sight. A heated argument had erupted inside the Ferrari between Dino and Anita. Suddenly, Dino slapped Anita brutally across her face.

She was stunned for a moment, as if she couldn't believe what had just happened. But then she immediately jumped out of the car, slammed the door loudly, and started walking very fast down the sidewalk. Dino was out of the car in an instant as well, and began running after her.

He caught up with her in a few seconds, grabbing her roughly by the arm. He tried to yank her back to the car, but stopped when he realized a small crowd of people was watching him.

"I'm sorry," Dino blurted out, just loud enough for the onlookers to hear. "I didn't mean it."

But Anita wasn't buying it. She yanked her arm back and hurried away.

At that moment, Dino's Ferrari screeched away from the curb. Juan the valet was behind the wheel as it roared down the street.

Dino began yelling at the other valets, "Hey! Tell Paco to bring that fucking car back!"

But all the other valets could do was shrug, and watch as Juan drifted around the next corner and went out of sight, leaving nothing behind but smoke spewing from the Ferrari's screaming tires.

Twenty-Two

▬▬▬▬▬▬

THE SUN WAS just setting when the Mustang roared across San Francisco's Bay Bridge.

Once the supercar was on the hilly streets of the city, it began passing streetcars and going around tight turns with speed and ease.

Night had fallen by the time Tobey pulled up in front of the Intercontinental Hotel. He parked in a restricted loading zone.

"You're twenty-three minutes late," Julia reminded him. "Hurry!"

Tobey leapt out of the car and headed for the door.

The lobby was brightly lit, glittering, and crowded. Tobey walked the length of it, anxious to find the room where Monarch said the details of the De Leon could be found. The race was going to be held the next morning.

If Tobey was going to participate, despite the dismal condition of the Mustang, he had to find the right room fast.

With his mind totally concentrating on the hotel room numbers, he turned a corner—and ran right into Dino.

The two rivals stopped in their tracks, stunned that they would meet this way. They glared at each other with pure hate and distrust.

At that moment, Tobey would have liked nothing better than to pummel Dino to death.

"Surprised you made it, Marshall," Dino said finally, the smarmy part of him taking over. "Impressed, actually . . ."

The situation was very tense. Dino could tell by the look in Tobey's eyes that a physical attack was probably seconds away.

He spoke again. "So, what's going on inside that head of yours, Tobey?"

"That you never went back for him," Tobey answered immediately. "That you left Pete back there to die."

Dino just smiled. "But I wasn't there," Dino said, goading him. "Remember? But I *was* there to comfort Anita at poor Pete's funeral and give her a shoulder to cry on, and much more after that. She's such a sweet, simple girl. But you already know that."

Tobey lost it. He grabbed Dino and slammed him hard against the wall.

But though Dino was startled at first, he recovered quickly and just smiled back at Tobey. He had the eyes of a psychopath.

"You really want to do this here, Marshall?" he asked

the enraged Tobey, looking around the crowded hotel. "Remember, one of us is on parole. But it's your move."

Tobey thought for a long moment. A fight here would bring the cops—and the cops would bring him to jail. If that happened, everything he had gone through in the past two days—and everything he'd been planning for the past two years—would have all been for nothing.

So he let his cooler side prevail. He stepped away from Dino.

"We'll settle this behind the wheel," he told him.

Dino just scoffed back at him. "Believe me, I'm not the slightest bit worried about you behind the wheel," he said.

"Really?" Tobey asked him. "Then why did you put that bounty on me?"

Dino's features fell. He was busted and he knew it. But he continued to taunt Tobey.

"Tomorrow is going to be fun," he said. "I'm glad I'm racing. I'm really looking forward to it."

"Is losing fun for you, Dino?" Tobey spit back at him. "Well, let me tell you something. When you're hanging upside down tomorrow, I'm not coming back for you."

Dino turned very dark. "Watch yourself, Tobey," he said. "I'm serious."

"I'll see you tomorrow, you pussy," Tobey told him.

Dino smirked. "I wouldn't be too sure of that," he said.

With that, Dino slowly backed down the hallway, Tobey watching his every move until he was finally out of sight.

*   *   *

Tobey climbed back into the Mustang a few minutes later.

He was seething. He pulled away from the hotel with a screech of tires and a burst of power.

Julia guessed correctly as to what had happened.

"You ran into him, didn't you?" she asked him. "That monster Dino."

Tobey didn't reply. He didn't have to.

"Listen," she went on, "just forget him. Let it go."

"That won't be easy," Tobey replied.

"Did you get the information you needed on the race?" she asked.

He nodded. "Yes—even though I was late."

"Then you just need to get out of this car," she said. "Take a hot shower, eat a good meal, and get some rest." She hit her iPad. "I'm going to book you a nice hotel room and—"

Tobey suddenly interrupted her. "You should stay with me," he said.

There was a long pause. For the first time in the trip Julia was authentically speechless.

"It would be safer that way," he added.

She looked at him and smiled.

And Tobey smiled back.

Then, suddenly . . . *Bam!*

An instant later, everything inside the Mustang was upside down, turning in wrenching slow motion. The car's airbags deployed and Julia was slammed hard by one inflating from the passenger's-side door. Tobey was yanked violently sideways, smashing his head on the driver's-side window. The Mustang was not only airborne; it was flipping over and over in midair. It seemed to take forever, but eventually it landed hard on its roof with a crash.

They'd been T-boned by a huge truck. Now, that truck had stopped. Inside was Big Al, Dino's number one goon. He admired his handiwork, then sped away down a side street.

Tobey regained consciousness to find himself upside down. He looked over at Julia and felt a crushing sensation in his chest. She was seriously hurt.

He reached down and hit the iPad. He called the Beast.

"We've been hit," he just barely managed to say. "Get here, now."

"We're on it," Joe Peck replied urgently.

Tobey unclipped his seat belt and fell to the roof. That's when Julia opened her eyes.

"Are you okay?" Tobey asked her.

"Get out," she told him weakly. "Go—before the police come."

Tobey kicked his door open, climbed out, and disappeared. Julia groaned softly, teetering on the brink of unconsciousness.

Suddenly her door was ripped open. A hand reached in, unclipped her seat belt, and gently took her out of the car.

It was Tobey.

He carried her to the middle of the street, leaving the carnage of the crash behind him.

The Beast appeared seconds later, roaring up to them. Finn immediately jumped out and, with Tobey's help, carefully placed Julia on the truck's rear seat.

They were lucky to find a hospital quickly.

The Beast screeched up to the emergency room entrance and Finn jumped out. He grabbed an EMT crew just returning from a drop-off. Finn found a gurney and Tobey carried Julia and put her on it, with the help of a female EMT.

"Finn, please stay with her," Tobey said.

"What's her name?" the female EMT asked. "Did she ever lose consciousness?"

"Her name is Julia," Tobey replied. "And she never loses consciousness. Ever. Trust me. Take good care of her."

Julia smiled weakly and fought back tears. Tobey watched as Finn and the female EMT wheeled her inside the hospital.

Then he turned back to the night.

Now, the gloves were off.

Twenty-Three

THE BAY BRIDGE was brightly lit up as usual, its reflection glowing off the water of San Francisco Bay.

Tobey was leaning on the bridge's railing, staring into the turbulent waters below. The Beast was parked nearby, engine idling. Joe Peck was inside, waiting patiently.

A taxicab pulled up beside him. Anita stepped out.

Joe watched silently as she walked toward Tobey. He just shook his head and whispered, "Tobey, dude, sometimes I wonder if you got a death wish, bro."

Anita and Tobey greeted each other in near silence. She leaned against the railing next to him. Heavy makeup covered her recently acquired black eye.

"You must be exhausted after what you've been through," she said to him.

"I'm okay," he replied.

"I know I probably look tired, too," she said.

Tobey smiled awkwardly—so did she. He began to say something about her black eye, but she cut him off.

"How are the guys?" she asked him instead. "I still miss them."

"Well, Benny's in jail," Tobey told her. "And Julia's in the hospital."

"I'm so sorry, Tobey," she said.

Their eyes locked.

"Why didn't you just leave him?" Tobey asked her. "He's a really bad guy."

"I know," she said. Then she held up her engagement ring. "And, I just did," she added.

Anita spotted Tobey's tattoo. She took his hand and turned it over so she could see it clearly.

Pete . . .

"I know now that Dino was there the night my brother died," Anita said after a while.

"Yeah, he was," Tobey replied with a nod.

"I wish I could give you those years back," Anita told him. "The time you spent in prison."

She moved closer to him—but he took a step back.

"I don't want the years back," he told her. "I just want that one moment back. Just one fucking moment . . ."

"It's not your fault," Anita told him. "Nothing would have kept Pete from getting in that car. Nothing . . ."

Tobey just shook his head. "Dino . . ." he said bitterly. "Dino could have just kept it between me and him."

"He's a scam artist," Anita said. "The whole thing was

a con. It started with the Mustang, then it turned into a shell game, moving this car here, that car there. But it went bust, and now he's broke. He owes a lot of money to a lot of people. Dangerous people. He's desperate. He needs to win De Leon or he'll lose everything."

"I lost you, my mother, my father, Pete, the shop . . ." Tobey said. "I lost everything."

"But Dino is willing to die," Anita said gravely.

"So am I," Tobey told her.

Anita studied him closely. She had no doubt he was serious.

"I need a car," he told her starkly. "The Mustang is wrecked."

Anita thought a moment. Then she began searching through her bag. She finally found a business card and handed it to Tobey.

"It's a warehouse," she told him. "That's the combination to the lock. I've never been inside, but I know Dino keeps some cars there."

Tobey studied the combination numbers on the business card.

"But, please, Tobey," she warned him. "Don't get too close to him. He's capable of anything."

Tobey smiled darkly.

"So am I," he said.

Twenty-Four

▬▬▬▬▬

IT WAS NOW the dead of night.

The junkyard was dark, full of shadows, and, hopefully, deserted.

Tobey and Joe Peck drove through the place in the Beast. Both were highly on guard.

"Boy, this feels like a setup," Joe said ominously.

Tobey didn't reply.

Up ahead they saw a dusty shed with a stack of crushed cars blocking its roll-up door. They stopped the Beast and got out.

Joe's flashlight found the shed's lock. Tobey immediately dialed in the combination numbers from the business card. The lock clicked open on the first try.

He rolled up the door and the flashlight revealed what was inside. Three cars hidden under blankets. Tobey and

Joe moved some old junk parts and boxes off the first one. The dust became thick as they pulled the blanket off. Underneath was a 1975 Ferrari Dino.

They were both awestruck. This was a fantastic, extremely expensive car.

Joe Peck blurted out: "Wow—Dino's got a Dino . . ."

But Tobey had already moved on to the second car. He pulled off its blanket. Beneath was a brand-new Porsche.

"That's a 911GT," Tobey exclaimed. "Big bucks for that, too."

They made their way to the last car. They both pulled the blanket off together.

Beneath was a Koenigsegg.

Tobey and Joe both froze in place. For them, this was like seeing a ghost.

"Damn," Joe breathed. "Could this be *the* car?"

Tobey knelt down and ran his hands over some scratches on the front bumper. They matched up with where scratches would be if this car had forced another off the road. At that moment, Tobey was convinced. This was the same car that had caused their friend's death.

Seeing it and knowing this was overwhelming for both Tobey and Joe.

"Why didn't he just destroy it?" Joe Peck asked. "Torch it? Do something to it. Here's all the evidence right here."

Tobey shook his head. He had no idea.

"Maybe it's hard to set two million dollars on fire?" he asked. "Or maybe he just thought he'd never get caught."

Joe smiled darkly.

"Well," he said. "He was wrong there."

A few minutes later, the silence of the junkyard was split by the roar of a hypercar coming to life. It sounded like a lion, warning anyone within earshot not to come any closer.

The Beast began pulling out the stack of junked cars that had been blocking the shed's doors. They moved like they were toys, opening a way through the wrecks.

Suddenly, the Koenigsegg rolled out, Tobey behind the wheel.

He gave the accelerator a few short stabs—and then sped off into the night.

Minutes later, Tobey was roaring through the streets of San Francisco, strapped in the powerful, ultra-expensive Koenigsegg sports car.

He rocketed through a red light without even noticing it. His thoughts were a million miles away. Just three days before, he was in prison serving the last hours of a sentence for killing one of his best friends—a crime he did not commit. Now he was driving the same car the real killer had used to end Little Pete's life. And with it, he intended teaching the real killer a lesson—or die trying.

But then, he saw the red light still glowing in his rearview mirror and immediately slowed down. It would not be good to be stopped by the cops at this point. That would send all his best-laid plans right down the drain.

He woke himself up mentally and started concentrating on what he was doing—and on what had to be done.

Minutes later, he pulled into the parking lot of the hospital. Climbing out of the Koenigsegg, he pulled his hoodie over his head and snuck in through a side entrance.

He quickly found the right corridor and saw Finn standing outside a hospital room. Finn put his finger to his lips, silently telling Tobey to stay quiet. The two friends pound-hugged, then Tobey went into Julia's room.

Julia was lying on the bed, hooked up to a gaggle of tubes, wires, and monitors.

She was asleep, but as soon as Tobey got close to her bed, she opened her eyes.

"How are you feeling?" he asked her quietly.

"Beat up," she replied. "But I'm fine."

"You are not the girl I thought you were," Tobey told her sincerely.

She smiled a little.

"You find out a lot about a person after they've been hit by a truck," she said.

Tobey smiled and Julia closed her eyes.

"What are you going to do tomorrow?" she asked him sleepily.

"I'm going to show up on time," he replied. "Ready to go."

"But you can't race in the De Leon," she said. "In what car?"

"I found a car," Tobey told her cryptically.

"And do I want to know where you got it?" she asked.

He shook his head. "No, you don't."

"Is it fast at least?" she asked him.

"Fast enough," he replied.

Julia smiled but was definitely nodding off.

"I'll let you sleep," Tobey told her.

"I don't want to sleep," she replied. "Not while you're here. I just spent forty-eight hours straight trying to get you to talk because . . . you're . . . you're . . ."

But she was quickly fading and couldn't get the words out.

"I'm what?" Tobey suddenly wanted to know.

But she seemed to go back to sleep. Tobey quietly stepped away from the bed.

"You're Mr. Strong and Silent . . ." she finally said, though more asleep than awake.

She smiled, eyes still closed. Tobey stepped back closer to the bed and leaned in close to her. She opened her eyes.

"How about you be Ms. Strong and Silent for a change?" he said.

Then he kissed her . . .

"Rest, okay?" he told her.

"Okay," she replied.

Tobey headed for the door, but then he heard her whisper.

"Tobey?" she said.

He turned back to her one more time.

"Yes?" he said.

She thought for a moment, then said, "Do it for Pete."

Part
Seven

Twenty-Five

IT WAS EARLY morning and somewhere up in the mountains of Mendocino a starting line had been established.

Three dozen people had gathered there, an exclusive club, each one invited personally by Monarch. They'd all been sworn to secrecy—this was how the De Leon was run. The most exciting street racing event in the world had more layers of security than a CIA black op.

In addition to the small crowd, there were a dozen or so car crewmembers, including Dino's support team. Big Al was there, too, along with his big-ass truck. A black leather bra was covering its huge chrome grille. The grille had sustained some minor front-end damage recently, but it was important that the evidence of that damage stayed hidden.

Watching all this activity was Monarch himself. The

mysterious maestro was still ensconced in his studio; its location was as top secret as the De Leon itself. He had a large bank of video monitors in front of him. They were beaming footage from the dozens of cameras he'd had stashed along the racecourse, its exact route unknown to anyone but him.

This was Monarch's baby, and he wasn't shy about letting everyone know it. Those in the immediate area were listening to him via a PA system set up at the starting line. Thousands more across the country and around the world were tuned in to his show as well. His voice swelled with both pride and audio volume whenever he spoke.

"This is by far the best De Leon I've ever put together," he bragged over the air. "This is my *David*, my *Pieta*, my *Soup Can*. My *Sistine Chapel*."

Then came a sudden rumbling sound. To the uninformed it was a startling noise—way too similar to how an earthquake sounded just before the ground opened up. After all, Mendocino *did* straddle the San Andreas Fault line. But this roar had a more mechanical origin. It was the sound of five supercars arriving at the De Leon starting line.

They were driving parade-style. First in line was the Saleen S7 Turbo, driven by a guy named Gooch. Hand-built and made mostly of carbon fiber, it was packing a 427-cubic-inch engine capable of kicking 800 horsepower or more. It also came arrayed with many scoops, spoilers, and other design tricks, all to make it as aerodynamic as possible.

The McLaren F-1 came next, driven by Texas Mike.

Dark gray and sinister-looking, it was actually a production car, and *not* hand-built. But it was also incredibly light and incredibly fast—no surprise as it boasted a 6.1 liter twelve-cylinder turbo-ized engine. Like a jet fighter, it had a rear aileron-type spoiler that moved automatically, depending on its speed.

Next came the Bugatti Veyron, driven by the gentleman of the race, a guy named English Paul. The Veyron looked like the offspring of a Volkswagen that'd had sex with something from the movie *Tron*. It had curves where other racers had sharp angles; it was round in places where other racers were square. With its highly polished bronze wheels and diamond-cut, glass-like body, it might have been the most glamorous car in the race.

The GTA Spano pulled in behind the Bugg. Driven by a guy named Johnny V, it was the perfect car for the De Leon because very little was known about it. It was built in Spain, and its creators had kept its existence top secret from the rest of the racing world until 2008, and even then, they only offered a peek. Its engine was a V-10 that kicked 820 horsepower and its body was made of carbon fiber, titanium, and Kevlar—the same material used in bulletproof vests. But beyond that, it was the phantom in the field.

Then came Dino's Lambo Elemento.

It was a very cool car—V-10 engine, sexy Italian shape, weighing barely 2,000 pounds, it was one of only a handful ever built. But cool car didn't automatically mean cool driver. Just the opposite in this case. Dino might have been a rock star at the Mount Kisco Drive-in, but here, at the very soul of the street racing universe, he was widely considered to be an asshole. His reputation for wrecking guys at Indy while under a caution flag preceded him. Racing was a brutal, sometimes heartless, sport. But bouncing a competitor when the yellow was out was considered extremely bad form. Even the fact that he'd won the De Leon the year before did not count for much with the crowd. As proof, when he arrived, some boos could be heard over the roar of his Elemento's engine.

The supercars began to maneuver themselves into their assigned slots at the starting line. Before them stretched a long, winding, hilly course, one that would need a combination of skills to conquer. Speed, of course, would be the number one factor. But steering, strategy, patience, and, most of all, guts would also be required. This would not be a closed track—like all street races, civilian vehicles would most likely be found driving on the course. In all likelihood a police car or two would probably show up, too.

"We have our lineup!" Monarch bellowed. "In the first row, we have English Paul in the Bugatti Veyron and Dino Brewster in his Lamborghini Elemento. Row two is Gooch in his Saleen S7 and Texas Mike in his McLaren F1. Third row and lonely is Johnny V in his GTA Spano. We're looking at seven million dollars in cars and horsepower here folks! Winner takes all—and the losers walk home."

* * *

The sun continued to rise. The air grew warmer. The race was about to start—but Tobey was not there.

Monarch had noticed.

"There is still no sign of Tobey Marshall," he told his listeners with just a minute to go. "Maybe this race won't have as much soap opera as we thought."

Sitting inside his Lamborghini, Dino smirked on hearing this.

"Chump," he thought aloud.

But Tobey *was* on his way.

At that moment, he was flying up the mountains in the Koenigsegg, tearing up the asphalt on the rapidly ascending roads. Once he was in earshot, his presence was quickly known.

"Hold on," Monarch told his listeners. "Do I hear a sixth car approaching? I can't really see who, but . . . stand by . . ."

When Monarch realized who it was, his voice went up another notch in volume and excitement.

"My people!" he announced. "Tobey Marshall has just arrived! And he's driving a Koenigsegg Agera! But hold on, my children—do the math with me—where's the Shelby Mustang? Or do we even care?"

Tobey rolled up to the starting line and let the crowd drink him in. He knew it didn't matter to Monarch or anyone else that he was here in a Koenigsegg and not the

Shelby. Just the opposite—it only added to the drama, the soap opera, which was what the De Leon and Monarch's followers thrived on.

But when Dino spotted the Koenigsegg, a soap opera was the farthest thing from his mind. He nearly voided himself on his hand-brushed Gallardo leather seats. Tobey was driving the car he should have burned a long time ago. Dino knew he'd been found out for sure now—and he knew there was only one person who could have snitched: Anita.

He actually thought aloud, "I had Big Al hit the wrong person."

Tobey eased the Koenigsegg into his assigned slot, last row, next to the GTA Spano. He looked down at the "Pete 392" tattoo on his arm and felt a kind of tranquility come over him. Finally, all the bullshit was over with. Everything he'd done in the past two years—and in the past two days—had led up to this moment. Despite all the obstacles, the cops, Dino, despite everything, here he was, ready to race.

This moment was what it was all about. For his mom, for his dad. For Julia. And most of all, for Pete. He tapped his tattoo twice for good luck and whispered: "Do or die little brother—this one's for you . . ."

Then came the words everyone had been waiting for. Monarch bellowed: "It's time, gentlemen . . ."

A portable dragster light grid had been put in place at the starting line. It held three yellow lights and one green.

The racers revved their engines to full peak now—the noise was the loudest so far.

Suddenly, the lights fell down the grid and the green light exploded in a puff of smoke.

The six cars screamed off the starting line.

The Bugatti was in first place in an instant, the other five cars right behind it. But the race almost ended before it could begin. The six supercars came very close to a massive pileup going into the first turn, which was a hard downhill right. Bunched together, door-to-door and tail to nose, they all took the corner like they were running on rails.

Watching intently on his remote video setup, Monarch began barking like an announcer at the Indy 500.

"English Paul in the Bugatti has taken the hole shot!" he yelled into his mic. "With Dino Brewster holding a tight second. Then we have Gooch's Saleen, Texas Mike's McLaren and Johnny V in the Spano. Bringing up the rear is little old Tobey Marshall. If the kid from Mount Kisco plans on winning this race, he'd better get his ass in gear!"

Hitting 120 mph already, the cars were so close together some of their mirrors were scraping each other. The noise, the fire, the smoke—it was all mind-blowing. Exploding out onto a straightaway, Tobey was shifting like a madman. His speedometer was climbing by the second . . . 125 . . . 145 . . . 175 . . . As much as he loved the Shelby Mustang, the Koenigsegg was frighteningly powerful. The adrenaline rush was incredible.

As the road rose ahead of him, Tobey settled in and started thinking strategy. He studied his nearest competitor: the GTA Spano, off to his right and just a few inches ahead. It was still early in the race, but he decided to make a move. He hit the gas and swerved right at the Spano. The sudden maneuver stunned Johnny V. He overreacted, sending him wide right and causing two of his wheels to go off the pavement.

Monarch saw the move and became very excited.

"Tobey Marshall and Johnny V are already battling for fifth!" he yelled. "Tobey is actually exchanging paint with the Spano, and wait . . . Johnny V is off the road!"

Tobey watched the GTA go sideways behind him. He didn't have time to think about it. He hit the gas again.

"Okay, Johnny V has recovered!" Monarch reported. "But Tobey has already moved up a notch. He's taken over fifth place!"

The racers were climbing a hill now, each driver with the gas pedal mashed, each waiting and wondering where the road went from there.

But, suddenly, a police helicopter appeared over the racecourse. It came out of the trees and was looking down on the supercars as they neared the top of the hill.

Monarch was incensed.

"Flying cops!" he shouted. "Like flies in my ointment, my children. The California Highway Patrol is in the air over our course!"

The police helicopter was a Bell 412, a powerful, agile machine. Nose down, it was flying at full tilt just twenty feet off the ground. It was almost as if it was signaling the racers that they'd been found out.

Monarch picked up a paperweight and hurled it against the wall of his secret studio.

"Someone snitched!" he bellowed. "Someone spilled the beans to the fuzz! They might have been thinking they were doing some good—but take it from me, you add cops to this race and people *will get hurt*!"

There was nothing the racers could do about the helicopter but keep going. They roared underneath the aircraft, all in a serpentine line, and at tremendous speed flew over the crest of the hill.

But the copter immediately climbed, did a smooth 180-degree turn, and took off after the racers.

Monarch was still supremely pissed.

"Racers should race," he yelled into his microphone, "and cops should eat doughnuts. This has just become a death race!"

With the GTA Spano no longer beside him, Tobey was able to take over the middle of the road. He was now directly behind the McLaren and the Saleen S7.

But as soon as he settled in behind them, two police cars appeared up ahead. Traveling side by side, lights flashing, sirens wailing, they were coming from the opposite direction and heading right at the racers.

Tobey knew this was more than just an ordinary race for him. Of them all, he had the most to lose if the cops stopped the De Leon and apprehended the drivers.

With this in mind, he became focused like never

before. It was almost as if he began seeing everything just a few seconds ahead of time. The McLaren and the Saleen were in front of him. When he sensed the McLaren might go wide to set up his next turn, Tobey saw another opportunity to make another move. He hit his brakes while going into the turn and began drifting violently between the McLaren and the Saleen S7. The object of his desire was a space right between them.

Monarch saw the gutsy maneuver and approved.

"Tobey Marshall is going to roll the dice!" he yelled. "He's trying to try to split the McLaren and the Saleen . . . Wow! . . . Ballsy!"

Tobey successfully squeezed himself between the McLaren and the Saleen. But he didn't want to stay there for long. They came up on a curve, still sandwiched together. But just when it came time to turn, Tobey hit the gas a second before Texas Mike did, and suddenly the McLaren was behind him. Just like that, Tobey was in fourth place.

"Marshall's balls have been located!" Monarch roared. "And they are large!"

Tobey felt good about his move, too. The Saleen was right in front of him with the McLaren right behind. But the two police cars were still heading right at the racers, with a convergence speed of more than 250 miles an hour. And no one was giving up their position.

Suddenly the race transformed into a massive game of chicken, with the six supercars coming from one direction and the two speeding police cars coming from the other.

Luckily, the cops blinked first.

At the very last instant, both cruisers jammed on their brakes and skidded to the side of the road. Clouds of burnt rubber filled the air as they tailspun themselves onto the dirt shoulder.

The supercars went by them like six gunshots. But the cops were not out of it. Both spun their cars around, gained the pavement again, and, sirens still screaming, began a pursuit.

A short distance up the road, an unsuspecting civilian car was traveling in the same direction as the racers. Coming up on it at lightning speed was the Bugatti and Dino's Lamborghini. Dino was drafting off English Paul and trying to time the moment before they both overtook the civilian car. But his indecision got the best of him. He swung out to pass the Bugatti, but acted too late. English Paul matched his speed and then some, closing the door on Dino. Slamming his fist against his steering wheel, Dino was forced back into second place.

But then more police interference came into play. The police helicopter appeared again, this time swooping in very low over the tops of the cars before heading farther down the racecourse. Once it was about a half mile in front of them, it suddenly pulled up into a hover. Then its pilot brought his aircraft down very low and went into a crab maneuver, flying sideways just a few feet off the pavement, essentially blocking the road.

"The cops are trying everything possible to stop my race!" Monarch yelled into his microphone. "Get that bird out of here! People will die. Let's hope English Paul doesn't back down."

The Bugatti was the first racer to come upon the copter—but English Paul showed no signs of slowing down. If anything, he started going faster. The helicopter pilot saw this and panicked. He jerked up on his controls and climbed a few feet just seconds before causing a devastating collision.

The Bugatti slid through the narrow space below the copter's landing skids. In rapid order, the other racers safely zoomed underneath the copter as well.

But the copter's crabbing maneuver had really just been a delaying tactic, a trick to throw off the racers. Because yet another police car was waiting up ahead. Its police officer was preparing to throw a spike strip across the road. Any tire hitting it would explode immediately. As the racers were traveling practically bumper to bumper and in excess of 150 mph at the moment, such a blowout would cause a catastrophic pileup.

The cop threw the spike strip out onto the asphalt nevertheless, just as the Bugatti was approaching. But again, English Paul was a real pro. Spying a narrow gap between the spikes and the cop who threw them, he expertly threaded the needle, zooming right through the tiny opening and scaring the cop half to death.

The rest of the cars followed the Bugatti's line and

avoided the strip as well. Another police tactic had been foiled.

Throughout all this Tobey was able to maintain his strong position and stay in fourth place. The farmlands of Mendocino were blurring by him now as he roared along at close to 160 mph, accelerating all the time. He hoped the cops would realize the futility of their tactics and just let them be.

But no such luck.

First one, then two, slowly moving police cars now appeared on the roadway, again heading right at the racers. These two were zigzagging back and forth in what law enforcement called a rolling road block. All the racers saw them and knew timing their way past them would be crucial in preventing another potential disaster.

The Bugatti was on them in seconds. In another display of fantastic driving, English Paul perfectly split the two zigzagging police cars. Dino went right behind him, mimicking the Bugatti's maneuver but coming very close to clipping both police cars in the process.

The Saleen S7 came rocketing by next. Gooch expertly moved around the path of the first cruiser in a loud screeching drift that was a success. But the maneuver put the Saleen directly into the path of the second cruiser, which was now blocking its path.

Doomed, Gooch had no other choice. He put the slanted front grille of the Saleen right under the second cruiser's fender and launched the cop car as if it were going off a ski jump. The cruiser went completely air-borne, spun around, and then came crashing to the ground. It skidded for a long time on its side before finally coming to a smoky, dusty halt, the cops inside mightily stunned.

The Saleen had taken a fatal blow, though. It bottomed out and ground to a halt in a shower of sparks and smoke.

Monarch came out of his seat.

"The Gooch has been taken out!" he roared. "He's completely gone! The Saleen is out because of police interference!"

Luckily Tobey saw the whole thing, again like it was happening in slow motion. He'd watched English Paul start his maneuver and how Dino followed him through. But then Gooch caught it—rather heroically, but abruptly ending his race. Tobey came up on the Saleen's crash just seconds after it happened but was able to rocket by the mayhem, bursting through the storm of smoke left by Gooch's demise.

When he could see daylight again, Tobey found himself in third place.

"British Paul still holds first," Monarch reported. "Dino is still in second, but Tobey Marshall has moved into third. We're down to five cars, people!"

Monarch was not only following the action on his video monitors. He was also hacking into the highway patrol's communications as they tried to disrupt the race. Most of what he heard was typical Smokey stuff—locations and status, with some bitching about how none of their tactics had worked so far. But then he heard something that chilled him right to the bone. In among the static and chatter, someone spoke three words: "Deadly force authorized."

Monarch thought to himself, *Are they going to start shooting at us?*

The racers left the rolling hills of coastal Mendocino and entered the famous Redwoods Forest.

They were stacked up again. Bumper to bumper, there was only a second between the Bugatti in the lead and the GTA bringing up the rear.

The police copter was still overhead, but its pilots could no longer see the supercars because of the thick canopy of gigantic trees. But this did not mean the racers would have smooth sailing.

Just the opposite.

Tobey rocketed through the forest, still in third, stuck on Dino's bumper. Suddenly he saw a bus in the lane straight ahead. At the same moment, a fully-loaded logging truck appeared, coming at the racers from the other direction.

The truck driver saw the handful of racers approaching at 150 mph and blew his horn—but it was too late. He gave a few feet on the side of the road—and it was enough for English Paul, Dino, and Tobey to roar through. But the McLaren, the bus, and the truck all crossed paths at the same time.

The McLaren's side mirrors shattered in twin explosions of glass and carbon fiber. That's how closely Texas Mike had to thread the needle between the bus and the truck. The maneuver seemed to last an eternity for him, but then he saw daylight and a long straightaway ahead of him and knew he was safely clear.

The truck driver had no such luck. His rig jackknifed, its trailer swinging around and unleashing its load of freshly cut trees. Huge logs bounced down the road, one of them sideswiping Johnny V's GTA Spano, causing him to lose control.

Then, at the worst possible moment, another police car suddenly appeared on the racetrack. It had been driving behind the logging truck, but an instant after the truck driver skidded, the cruiser crashed head-on into the GTA Spano.

Monarch was livid.

"The Spano just took a cop car to the face!" he yelled into his microphone. "Our thoughts and prayers are with you, Johnny V! The winner's prize is getting smaller because we only have four cars left!"

The remaining supercars raced through the strobing Redwoods Forest. They were rocketing along, all in a line, over the two-lane blacktop, at 185 mph.

But up ahead, law enforcement had yet another obstacle waiting for them—the first after Monarch had intercepted the "deadly force authorized" message.

An empty cruiser had been hidden behind a huge red-wood tree. Its engine was turned on and its accelerator was racing madly. The pack of racers, still flying along with just millimeters separating them, were unknowingly heading toward this hidden, empty cruiser, English Paul's Bugatti still in the lead.

Just an instant before the pack arrived, a cop standing nearby reached into the cruiser. His billy club had been keeping the gas pedal jammed to the floor. Now he put the car's transmission into drive and murderously launched the cruiser right into the path of the oncoming racers.

English Paul almost made it past the driverless cruiser; his car's tremendous speed almost came through. But his back end was clipped by the cruiser's front end, and the Bugatti simply exploded. The momentum from the blast sent the car spinning off the road and into the forest, where it pinballed off several of the ancient trees before finally coming to a fiery, smoky halt.

Monarch was incensed. Suddenly he knew what "deadly force" meant.

He told his listeners, "The Bugatti just got taken out by an empty police car. The cops are playing dirty and they're playing God. And it's not right, my children."

But as so often happens in racing, one driver's tragedy was another driver's opportunity. And so it was for Tobey.

A moment before the Bugatti got wrecked, Dino had stood on his brakes and gone wide, avoiding becoming entangled in the carnage. It showed some outstanding driving on Dino's part, but it was exactly what Tobey had been waiting for.

Instead of hitting his brakes and mimicking Dino, Tobey stood on his accelerator instead and split the gap between the Elemento and the leftovers of the Bugatti wreck.

It all happened in a flash. It was so quick, Tobey actually closed his eyes in the last instant of this maneuver—it was that tight and dangerous.

But when he opened his eyes again, he was in first place.

And Monarch was excited again.

"Tobey Marshall is running first!" he yelled. "The blue-collar kid from Mount Kisco is very close to wearing Cinderella's slipper!"

An instant later, Tobey exited the Redwoods Forest. He was topping 175 mph and heading for the Pacific Coast Highway. Behind him was the McLaren, and behind the McLaren was a very pissed-off Dino.

The road split in two here—one direction went straight, and the other went to the left. Tobey drifted left at 160 mph, knowing that's where the finish line lay. Texas Mike and Dino did the same thing. But they also spotted four police cars coming straight at them before they turned.

These police cars joined the others, and now there was an all-out chase on the racecourse. A half-dozen cruisers were in pursuit of the remaining race cars.

But Monarch was on top of it.

"Most cop cars top out at one thirty, max," he told his listeners angrily. "My racers go almost twice that. So good luck catching up, Smokey. We'll let you know who wins."

Thousands of people all over the world were following the race via Monarch's broadcast.

Benny was one of them. He was in a military jail cell in Nevada, along with the rest of the crew of the purloined Super Stallion helicopter. They were all charged with misuse of government property. But they had all become great friends by this time, and Benny had made street racing fans out of all of them. Their guards had let them listen to Monarch's play-by-play on Benny's iPad, and the copter crew was cheering just as loudly as Benny anytime Tobey made a move.

Joe Peck and Finn were also listening in. They were in the Beast, parked in the hospital lot right outside Julia's hospital room, cheering on their friend while staying close to her, because they knew that's what Tobey would want them to do.

The huge audience also included Julia herself, who, though still in her hospital bed, was recovering at a rapid pace. She was listening to Monarch's broadcast on her laptop, and she was screaming like a banshee at every turn of the race, even more so than the Marshall Motors team.

"C'mon, Tobey!" she'd cried over and over. "Push it! Get there! *Push it!*"

She'd taken to steering the laptop as if it were the wheel

of Tobey's car. She was even leaning right and left at all the curves, as if she was right there in the car with him.

Her screams got so loud, they eventually brought the floor nurse hurrying into her room, thinking something was wrong.

"Sorry about that," Julia apologized to her. "It's just that a friend of mine—or, I should say, a *very* good friend of mine—is in a car race right now, and he's in the lead. It's very exciting."

The nurse looked at her skeptically.

"Is it your boyfriend?" she asked.

Julia began to answer, but then stopped herself for a second.

"Well, at the moment," she finally replied, "I think he considers me just a little bit more than a good right-seater."

The nurse rolled her eyes, checked Julia's monitors, and then turned to go.

"Any girl who screams like that for a guy?" she said over her shoulder. "Honey, you better make sure he's your boyfriend."

The three surviving race cars were now flying down the Pacific Coast Highway.

Their drivers weren't paying any attention to the beautiful scenery, though. Such things as pounding surf and the sparkling ocean tend to get lost at 170 mph.

Tobey was still in the lead, and Dino was still in third

place. But he'd managed to creep up on the second-place McLaren. Suddenly he was right on Texas Mike's left fender. They went into a hard right-hand corner and actually hit each other.

Then they came to a vicious hairpin turn. Tobey went through smoothly, but drifting side by side, Dino brutally swerved into the McLaren. Texas Mike lost control, steered too wide outside the line, and went over the embankment. His McLaren began tumbling at more than 110 mph. There was another storm of fire and sparks as the car was quickly demolished.

Monarch was right on the crash.

"Rubbin' might be racin'," he reported. "But Texas Mike just got barbequed . . . Dino Brewster just flicked him and the McLaren into a roll. You know what this means, my children? This race is now definitely personal between the last two men standing."

Tobey saw the McLaren wreck in his rearview mirror. When the smoke cleared, Dino's Lambo was suddenly just two car lengths behind him. And behind Dino were at least six police cars in very hot pursuit.

Dino quickly closed the gap on Tobey. In seconds, he was in the exact same position he'd been that night he'd killed Little Pete. Tobey had no trouble seeing Dino in his rearview mirror. He could almost reach out and touch him. His rival's face was a mask of pure anger.

Tobey knew Dino well. He knew his rival was desperate at that moment—for money, for revenge, even to destroy evidence. This meant he was capable of doing anything.

As Tobey had predicted, an instant later, Dino made his move. He tried to force the Koenigsegg off the road. But Tobey had been waiting for the maneuver and countered it immediately—but in a highly unusual way. Instead of hitting the gas and trying to get away, he slammed on his brakes instead, allowing Dino to streak by him.

Monarch was confused—and so were his thousands of listeners around the globe.

"Tobey Marshall just let Dino get by him!" Monarch shouted like a madman. "Wake up, Tobey! Wake up and smell that two-million-dollar Lambo in your pocket! My people?! My children! It's a two-man duel to the finish . . ."

But no sooner had Dino gone by him when Tobey immediately pulled in behind him. Now he was riding the Lambo's rear bumper.

Dino looked in his mirror and quickly realized what Tobey was doing. The tables had been turned. Now *he* was suddenly in the same vulnerable position that Little Pete had found himself in the night he died. The front of Tobey's Koenigsegg was just an inch away from Dino's back bumper, even as both cars were going in excess of 190 mph. A towering lighthouse was just up ahead. That was the finish line. It was literally right around the next corner.

Tobey gripped the wheel as tight as he could and smiled grimly. He'd finally achieved a long and dark goal. All those days in prison, the solitary weeks and months, saying his prayer, doing his push-ups—just hoping he'd have a chance to be where he was at that exact moment. To make Dino feel exactly how Little Pete felt seconds before his death.

But now what? He was here. He'd reached his objective. But what did it mean? And what should he do next?

He whispered, "Pete, if you're with me, I need you to tell me what to do."

His RPMs redlined at that moment. He was going flat-out, more than 220 mph.

Suddenly Tobey cut his car across the back of Dino's draft. This served to slingshot the Koenigsegg along to the other side of the Lambo.

Dino saw this and thought he'd died and gone to heaven. He immediately swerved right into Tobey's path in a bid to take him out once and for all . . .

And there it was: all those hours and days Tobey had spent reliving every racing move he'd ever made—it all came flooding back to him. Pete was speaking to him from on high.

Suddenly, Tobey knew exactly what to do.

He slammed on his brakes again. This forced Dino to slide in front of him—and right across the road. The Lambo hit the gravel shoulder at tremendously high speed, and the lack of traction sent it flipping over and over—and over. Finally landing on its roof, it slid right up to the edge of the cliff, where it burst into flames.

Monarch could not contain himself.

"Dino took a swing!" he yelled. "And he missed because Tobey was ready for it! Dino has flipped his

Elemento! Dino Brewster is out! Down goes Dino! Down goes Dino! Tobey Marshall is the last man standing. He's going to win the De Leon!"

It was all Tobey could do to keep his cool. He'd watched Dino's crash in his rearview mirror. He saw the Lambo catch on fire, creating a cloud of thick black smoke almost instantly. He saw the flames begin to devour Dino's car.

"Monarch Mania!" Monarch kept shouting. "This is the most insane De Leon ever run . . . I've had some wrecks in years past—but here? Every car but one is gone! This Marshall kid will make a milk run home to victory . . ."

But suddenly Tobey was feeling very strange. Yes, he'd accomplished his goal and more—basically he'd allowed Dino to kill himself. But nothing he'd done in prison had prepared him for *this* moment. The moment *after* his supposed triumph.

Dino was burning to death, just as Little Pete had burned. And it had been Dino's own fault; his own desperate ego had caused his horrific crash. But what should Tobey do now?

He suddenly swore at himself in a very loud voice, "You didn't figure out *everything*, you dickhead!"

Then in less than a half second, he whipped the Koenigsegg supercar into a 180-degree turn and headed back to Dino's wreck.

Monarch couldn't believe what he was seeing.

"Wait a moment," he told his followers. "What the hell is going on down there? Are my eyes deceiving me?"

Tobey skidded to a stop near the wrecked Lambo and jumped out. Pulling off his jacket, he ran toward the driver's side of the nearly totally engulfed car, hearing Dino's cries for help. Using the jacket for protection, he reached into the flames, grabbed Dino by his leather jacket, and roughly pulled him out of the wreck.

Monarch was flabbergasted.

"Tobey, what are you doing to me?" he yelled. "You are a half mile from the finish! Go to the lighthouse, kid! Go to the lighthouse!"

Tobey dragged his dazed rival about twenty feet from the burning car, pulling him up into a sitting position and letting him suck in some clean fresh air.

"Are you okay?" Tobey asked him. "Are you hurt?"

Dino just shook his head. "I'm okay," he said, just barely able to talk. "I'm okay . . ."

"That's good," Tobey said. "Because Pete says hello."

Tobey reared back and delivered a massive right cross to Dino's head. He'd never hit anyone so hard before, inside prison or out. It was so powerful Dino was slammed face-first into the pavement.

Then Tobey heard something in the near distance. Sirens. Coming on fast.

He hustled back to the Koenigsegg just as the police cars arrived on the scene. Two stopped near where Dino lay; four more continued their pursuit of Tobey.

He jumped back into the Koenigsegg and floored it. He just about literally flew toward the lighthouse—the police right on his tail.

He breathed in deeply. He knew *now* was the time to focus on what he did best. That is, driving flawlessly at the speed of light.

He crossed the finish line just moments later. That's all it took. It went by in a flash but he felt Pete was with him at that moment. Sitting right next to him, laughing as usual.

He'd completed his friend's vision. After all that had happened, *that* was the most important thing of all.

Tobey simply parked the car and waited. The police cars screeched up in back of him, surrounding him with sirens and flashing lights. He put his hands out the window, then opened the door and got out.

He lay down on the ground spread eagle, to make it easier for the cops to handcuff him.

He was beat up, dirty, sweaty, had burns on his hands, and was completely exhausted. And he was under arrest.

But . . . there was a smile on his face.

A short time later, Monarch finished his final broadcast for the De Leon. His voice was cool, calm, and collected—not the usual state of affairs for him.

"Tobey Marshall won the De Leon," he began. "And he was rewarded not with seven million dollars' worth of supercars, but with police bracelets. Yup. They cuffed him and stuffed him. And Dino Brewster will also be staring at a prison ceiling for many years. We just learned Dino got implicated in the racing death of Pete Coleman and also for running some sleazy Ponzi scheme. So Dino? Don't drop the soap, pretty boy. Wow—all those cars were wrecked and impounded. The police destroyed my *Mona Lisa*. Oh, Mona . . . But I can make a new Mona, and I will. De Leon lives! So until next time, my loyal subjects, keep the need. Keep the goddamn mutha-fucking need . . . for speed."

Monarch turned off his microphone and clapped his hands once in satisfaction.

He liked being a man of mystery. He really had been an F1 driver years before. He'd run at all the hot tracks around the world and had been hugely successful. In fact, he was probably *too* good at it, because he'd actually damaged his heart from taking too many risks and having too many adrenaline rushes. Or at least that's what his doctors told him.

Since then, he'd supported at least one team in every major car race around the world, but mostly because that's what his old-money family wanted him to do.

But secretly he'd also been supporting his true love—street racing. And he would do anything to see it prosper.

That's what his show and the De Leon were all about.

He stood up now and walked out from behind his console. His friends the seagulls were cawing madly at that moment. Usually he'd shoo them away—they loved his lighthouse retreat, but while he was on the air, they could be distracting. But now, with the show over for a while, they could cry as much as they wanted.

He walked out of the studio and out onto the lighthouse's balcony. He looked out over the sparkling ocean. It was deep blue, and rolling with waves—but not really high ones. Certainly not surfers' waves. This was not the Pacific. Monarch was looking out over the Atlantic.

He leaned against the railing and drank in the warmth of the midafternoon sun.

"Ah, there's nothing like this," he said. "Nothing like the great state of Maine."

Twenty-Six

TOBEY'S SENTENCE TURNED out to be a light one.

This time he took the plea bargain and settled for six months for grand theft auto.

It was not so bad. He'd been assigned to the minimum-security wing of a San Francisco area prison. There was no solitary this time. No drama. No prayers. No gang fights. Just a lot of time sitting around and talking to the other convicted auto thieves about all things cars, and all things street racing.

But he vowed that once he got out this time, he would stay out for good.

He was sitting at a table in the visitors' room, as he did every Wednesday at exactly 1:00 p.m.

The doors finally opened and Julia walked in, as she did every visitors' day, more gorgeous than ever.

And like every day when they met, he started off the conversation with three simple words: "You look beautiful."

As always Julia melted—but today it only lasted for a moment. Then she was all business.

"I talked to Ingram," she said. "He says you still owe him. He wants to have lunch to figure out some arrangement. I think there might be a driving assignment in it for you."

"Well, I can do lunch in, let's see, about a hundred and fifty days," Tobey said.

"I'll set it up," she replied without missing a beat.

"But remember," he told her. "First, we gotta go get Benny out of jail in Nevada. They take helicopter theft very seriously out there. He'll be getting sprung around the same time as me. We'll have to set up a rendezvous with the Beast."

"You realize that's seven hundred and fifty miles from here," Julia told him.

"Sounds like we're going to need a fast car," Tobey said.

"I already got it," she told him with a smile.

And just about 150 days later, Tobey walked out of the prison.

He was greeted at the gate by the roar of a lot of

horsepower. Then a true work of art pulled up in front of him. It was a 2015 Mustang GT.

Julia rolled down the window.

"Get in," she told him.

But Tobey just shook his head.

"No way," he said. "I've seen you drive."

A minute later, the Mustang growled to life again. Tobey was behind the wheel, hammering the throttle; Julia was in the passenger's seat.

He performed a great screech by aggressively turning the tires with his foot on the brake. It sounded like a symphony to him.

Then he let the brakes go and the wheels finally grabbed and they flew down the desolate road that lined the prison's perimeter, heading for the open highway beyond.